The Lady's Walk

by

Mrs. Oliphant

The Lady's Walk
by Mrs. Oliphant

Copyright © 2023

All Rights reserved.

ISBN: 978-93-60464-45-5

Published by

DOUBLE 9 BOOKS

2/13-B, Ansari Road
Daryaganj, New Delhi – 110002
info@double9books.com
www.double9books.com
Tel. 011-40042856

ABOUT THE AUTHOR

Margaret Oliphant Wilson Oliphant was a Scottish author and historical writer who usually wrote under the name Mrs. Oliphant. She was born Margaret Oliphant Wilson on April 4, 1828, and died on June 20, 1897. She writes "domestic realism, the historical novel, and tales of the supernatural" as her short stories. Margaret Oliphant was born in Wallyford, near Musselburgh, East Lothian. She was the only daughter and youngest child still living of Margaret Oliphant (1789–17 September 1854) and Francis W. Wilson, a clerk. We lived in Lasswade, Glasgow, and Liverpool when she was a child. In Wallyford, a street called Oliphant Gardens is named after her. As a girl, she was always trying new things with writing. Passages in the Life of Mrs. Margaret Maitland, her first book, came out in 1849. This was about the mostly successful Scottish Free Church movement, which was something her folks agreed with. Next came Caleb Field in 1851, the same year she met publisher William Blackwood in Edinburgh and was asked to write for Blackwood's Magazine. She did so for the rest of her life and wrote over 100 articles, including one that criticized Arthur Dimmesdale in Nathaniel Hawthorne's "The Scarlet Letter."

CONTENTS

CHAPTER I

I WAS on a visit to some people in Scotland when the events I am about to relate took place. They were not friends in the sense of long or habitual intercourse; in short, I had met them only in Switzerland in the previous year; but we saw a great deal of each other while we were together, and got into that easy intimacy which travelling brings about more readily than anything else. We had seen each other in very great *déshabillé* both of mind and array in the chilly mornings after a night's travelling, which perhaps is the severest test that can be applied in respect to looks, and amid all the annoyances of journeys short and long, with the usual episodes of lost luggage, indifferent hotels, fusses of every description, which is an equally severe test for the temper; and our friendship and liking (I am at liberty to suppose it was mutual, or they would never have invited me to Ellermore) remained unimpaired. I have always thought, and still think, that Charlotte Campbell was one of the most charming young women I ever met with; and her brothers, if not so entirely delightful, were nice fellows, capital to travel with, full of fun and spirit. I understood immediately from their conversation that they were members of a large family. Their allusions to Tom and Jack and little Harry, and to Mab and Mary, might perhaps have been tedious to a harsher critic; but I like to hear of other people's relations, having scarcely any of my own. I found out by degrees that Miss Campbell had been taken abroad by her brothers to recover from a long and severe task of nursing, which had exhausted her strength. The little ones had all been down with scarlet fever, and she had not left them night or day. "She gave up seeing the rest of us and regularly shut herself in," Charley informed me, who was the younger of the two. "She would only go out for her walk when all of us were out of the way. That was the worst of it," the young fellow said, with great simplicity. That his sister should give herself up to the nursing was nothing remarkable; but that she should deny herself their precious company was a heroism that went to her brother's heart. Thus by the way I learned a great deal about the family. Chatty, as they called her, was the sister-mother, especially of the little ones, who had been left almost in her sole charge since their mother died many years before. She was not a girl, strictly speaking. She was in the perfection of her womanhood and youth—about eight-and-twenty, the age when something of the composure of maturity has lighted upon the sweetness of the earlier years, and being so old enhances all the charm of being so young. It is chiefly among young married women that one sees this gracious and beautiful type, delightful to every sense and every requirement of the mind; but when it is to be met with unmarried it is more celestial still. I cannot but think with reverence that this delicate maternity and maidenhood—the perfect bounty of the one, the undisturbed grace of the other—has been the foundation of that adoring devotion which in the old days brought so many saints to the shrine of the Virgin Mother. But why I should thus enlarge upon Charlotte Campbell at the beginning of this story I can scarcely tell, for she is not the foremost figure in it, and I am unintentionally deceiving the reader to begin with.

They asked me to come and see them at Ellermore when we parted, and, as I have nothing in the way of a home warmer or more genial than chambers in the Temple, I accepted, as may be supposed, with enthusiasm. It was in the first week of June that we parted, and I was invited for the end of August. They had "plenty of grouse," Charley said, with a liberality of expression which was pleasant to hear. Charlotte added, "But you must be prepared for a homely life, Mr. Temple, and a very quiet one." I replied, of course, that if I had chosen what I liked best in the world it would have been this combination, at which she smiled with an amused little shake of her head. It did not seem to occur to her that she herself told for much in the matter. What they all insisted upon was the "plenty of grouse," and I do not pretend to say that I was indifferent to that.

Colin, the eldest son, was the one with whom I had been least familiar. He was what people call reserved. He did not talk of everything as the others did. I did not indeed find out till much later that he was constantly in London, coming and going, so that he and I might have seen much of each other. Yet he liked me well enough. He joined warmly in his brother's invitation. When Charley said there was plenty of grouse, he added, with the utmost friendliness, "And ye may get a blaze at a stag." There was a flavour of the North in the speech of all; not disclosed by mere words, but by an occasional diversity of idiom and change of pronunciation. They were conscious of this and rather proud of it than otherwise. They did not say Scotch, but Scots; and their accent could not be represented by any of the travesties of the theatre, or what we conventionally accept as the national utterance. When I attempted to pronounce after them, my own ear informed me what a travesty it was.

It was to the family represented by these young people that I was going when I started on August 20, a blazing summer day, with dust and heat enough to merit the name of summer if anything ever did. But when I arrived at my journey's end there was just change enough to mark the line between summer and autumn: a little golden haze in the air, a purple bloom of heather on the hills, a touch here and there upon a stray branch, very few, yet enough to swear by. Ellermore lay in the heart of a beautiful district full of mountains and lochs within the Highland line, and just on the verge of some of the wildest mountain scenery in Scotland. It was situated in the midst of an amphitheatre of hills, not of any very exalted height, but of the most picturesque form, with peaks and couloirs like an Alpine range in little, all glowing with the purple blaze of the heather, with gleams upon them that looked like snow, but were in reality water-white threads of mountain torrents. In front of the house was a small loch embosomed in the hills, from one end of which ran a cheerful little stream, much intercepted by boulders, and much the brighter for its interruptions, which meandered through the glen and fell into another loch of greater grandeur and pretensions. Ellermore itself was a comparatively new house, built upon a fine slope of lawn over the lake, and sheltered by fine trees—great beeches which would not have done discredit to Berkshire, though that is not what we expect to see in Scotland, besides the ashes and firs which we are ready to acknowledge as of northern growth. I was not prepared for the luxuriance of the West Highlands—the mantling green of ferns and herbage everywhere, not to say the wealth of flowers, which formed a centre of still more brilliant colour and cultivation amid all the purple of the hills. Everything was soft and rich and warm about the Highland mansion-house. I had expected stern scenery and a grey atmosphere. I found an almost excessive luxuriance of vegetation and colour everywhere. The father of my friends received me at a door which was constantly open, and where it seemed to me after a while that nobody was ever refused admission. He was a tall old man, dignified but homely, with white hair and moustache and the fresh colour of a rural patriarch; which, however, he was not, but an energetic man of business, as I afterwards found. The Campbells of Ellermore were not great chiefs in that much-extended clan, though they were perfectly well-known people and had held their little estate from remote antiquity. But they had not stood upon their gentility, or refused to avail themselves of the opportunities that came in their way. I have observed that in the great and wealthy region of which Glasgow is the capital the number of the irreconcilables who stand out against trade is few. The gentry have seen all the advantages of combining commerce with tradition. Had it not been for this it is likely that Ellermore would have been a very different place. Now it was overflowing with all those signs of care and simple luxury which make life so smooth. There was little show, but there was a profusion of comfort. Everything rolled upon velvet. It was perhaps more like the house of a rich merchant than of a family of long descent. Nothing could be more perfect as a pleasure estate than was this little Highland property. They had "plenty of grouse," and also of trout in a succession of little lochs and mountain streams. They had deer on the hills. They had their own mutton, and everything vegetable that was needed for the large, profuse household, from potatoes and cabbage up to grapes and peaches. But with all this primitive wealth there was not much money got out of Ellermore. The "works" in Glasgow supplied that. What the works were I have never exactly found out, but they afforded occupation for all the family, both father and sons; and that the results were of the most pleasing description as regarded Mr. Campbell's banker it was easy to see.

They were all at home with the exception of Colin, the eldest son, for whose absence many apologies, some of which seemed much more elaborate than were at all necessary, were made to me. I was, for my own part, quite indifferent to the absence of Colin. He was not the one who had interested me most; and though Charley was considerably younger than myself, I had liked him better from the first. Tom and Jack were still younger. They were well occupied at "the works," and came home only from Saturday to Monday. The little trio in the nursery were delightful children. To see them gathered about Charlotte was enough to melt any heart. Chatty, they called her, which is not a very dignified name, but I got to think it the most beautiful in the world as it sounded all over that cheerful, much-populated house. "Where is Chatty?" was the first question everyone asked as he came in at the door. If she was not immediately found, it went volleying through the house, all up the stairs and through the passages — "Chatty! where are you?" — and was always answered from somewhere or other in a full, soft voice, which was audible everywhere though it never was loud. "Here am I, boys," she would say, with a pretty inversion which pleased me. Indeed, everything pleased me in Chatty — too much, more than reason. I found myself thinking what would become of them all if, for example, she were to marry, and entered into a hot argument with myself on one occasion by way of proving that it would be the most selfish thing in the world were this family to work upon Chatty's feelings and prevent her from marrying, as most probably, I could not help feeling, they would. At the same time, I perceived with a little shudder how entirely the whole thing would collapse if by any chance Chatty should be decoyed away.

I enjoyed my stay beyond description. In the morning we were out on the hills or about the country. In the evening it very often happened that we all strolled out after dinner, and that I was left by Chatty's side, "the boys" having a thousand objects of interest, while Mr. Campbell usually sat in his library and read the newspapers, which arrived at that time either by the coach from Oban or by the boat. In this way I went over the whole "policy," as the grounds surrounding a country house are called in Scotland, with

Chatty, who would not be out of reach at this hour, lest her father should want her, or the children. She would bid me not to stay with her, when no doubt it would be more amusing for me to go with the boys; and when I assured her my pleasure was far greater as it was, she gave me a gracious, frank smile, with a little shake of her head. She laughed at me softly, bidding me not to be too polite or think she would mind if I left her; but I think, on the whole, she liked to have me with her in her evening walk.

"There is one thing you have not told me of," I said, "and that you must possess. I cannot believe that your family has been settled here so long without having a ghost."

She had turned round to look at me, to know what it was that had been omitted in her descriptions. When she heard what it was she smiled a little, but not with the pleasant mockery I had expected. On the contrary, it was a sort of gentle smile of recognition of something left out.

"We don't call it a ghost," she said. "I have wondered if you had never noticed. I am fond of it, for my part; but then I have been used to it all my life. And here we are, then," she added, as we reached the top of a little ascent and came out upon a raised avenue, which I had known by its name of the Lady's Walk, without as yet getting any explanation what that meant. It must have been, I supposed, the avenue to the old house, and now encircled one portion of the grounds without any distinct meaning. On the side nearest the gardens and house it was but slightly raised above the shrubberies, but on the other side rose to the summit of a high bank, sloping steeply to the river, which, after it escaped from the loch, made a wide bend round that portion of the grounds. A row of really grand beeches rose on each side of the path, and through the openings in the trees the house, the bright gardens, the silvery gleam of the loch were visible. The evening sun was slanting into our eyes as we walked along; a little soft yet brisk air was pattering among the leaves, and here and there a yellow cluster in the middle of a branch showing the first touch of a cheerful decay. "Here we are, then." It was a curious phrase; but there are some odd idioms in the Scotch—I mean Scots—form of our common language, and I had become accustomed now to accept them without remark.

"I suppose," I said, "there must be some back way to the village or to the farmhouse under this bank, though there seems no room for a path?"

"Why do you ask?" she said, looking at me with a smile.

"Because I always hear someone passing along—I imagine down there. The steps are very distinct. Don't you hear them now? It has puzzled me a good deal, for I cannot make out where the path can be."

She smiled again, with a meaning in her smile, and looked at me steadily, listening, as I was. And then, after a pause, she said, "That is what you are asking for. If we did not hear them it would make us unhappy. Did you never hear why this was called the Lady's Walk?"

When she said these words I was conscious of an odd enough change in my sensations—nay, I should say in my very sense of hearing, which was the one appealed to. I had heard the sound often, and, after looking back at first to see who it was and seeing no one, had made up my mind that the steps were on some byway out of sight and came from below. Now my hearing changed, and I could not understand how I had ever thought anything else; the steps were on a level with us, by our side—as if some third person were accompanying us along the avenue. I am no believer in ghosts, nor the least superstitious, so far as I had ever been aware (more than everybody is), but I felt myself get out of the way with great celerity and a certain thrill of curious sensation. The idea of rubbing shoulders with something unseen gave me a shock in spite of myself.

"Ah," said Charlotte, "it gives you an—unpleasant feeling. I forgot you are not used to it like me."

"I am tolerably well used to it, for I have heard it often," I said. It was cowardly to get to the other side, but I fear I did so with an involuntary movement. Then I laughed, which I felt to be altogether out of place and fictitious, and said, "No doubt there is some very easy explanation of it— some vibration or echo. The science of acoustics clears up many mysteries."

"There is no explanation," Chatty said almost angrily. "She has walked here far longer than anyone can remember. It is an ill sign for us Campbells when she goes away. She was the eldest daughter, like me; and I think she has got to be our guardian angel. There is no harm going to happen as long as she is here. Listen to her!" she cried, standing still with her hand raised. The low sun shone full on her, catching her brown hair, the lucid clearness of her brown eyes, her cheeks so clear and soft, in colour a little summer-brown too. I stood and listened with a something of excited feeling which I could not control. If I had followed my first impulse I am not sure that I should not have bolted through the shrubbery; but of course I did not. And the sound of this third person, whose steps were not to be mistaken though she was unseen, made my heart beat. It was no doubt the utmost folly; for there must be an explanation for it in nature: of that I could not doubt for a moment.

"You are startled," she said, with a smile.

"Well, I should not be acting my part, should I, as I ought, if I did not feel the proper thrill. It must be disrespectful to a ghost not to be afraid."

"Don't say a ghost," said Chatty; "I think *that* is disrespectful. It is the Lady of Ellermore; everybody knows about her. And do you know," she added, "when my mother died—the greatest grief I have ever known—the steps ceased? Oh, it is true! You need not look me in the face as if there was anything to laugh at. It is ten years ago, and I was only a silly sort of girl, not much good to anyone. They sent me out to get the air when she was lying in a doze; and I came here. I was crying, as you may suppose, and at first I did not pay any attention. Then it struck me all at once—the Lady was away. They told me afterwards that was the worst sign. It is always death that is coming when she goes away."

The pathos of this incident confused all my attempts to touch it with levity, and we went on for a little without speaking, during which time it is almost unnecessary to say that I was listening with all my might to those strange footsteps, which finally I persuaded myself were no more than echoes of our own.

"It is very curious," I said politely. "Of course you were greatly agitated and too much absorbed in real grief to have any time to think of any explanation—the state of the atmosphere perhaps"—

She gave me an indignant look. We were nearly at the end of the walk, and at that moment I could have sworn that the footsteps, which had got a little in advance, here turned and met us coming back. I am aware that nothing could sound more foolish, and that it could only be some vibration or atmospheric phenomenon. But yet this was how it seemed: it was not an optical but an aural delusion. So long as the steps were going with us it was less impossible to account for it; but when they turned and audibly came back to meet us! Not all my strength of mind could prevent me from springing aside to let them pass. This time they came directly between us, and the agility of my start and withdrawal was naturally much more significant than the faltering laugh with which I excused myself. "It is a very curious sound indeed," I said, with a tremor which slightly affected my voice.

Chatty gave me a reassuring smile. She did not laugh at me, which was consolatory. She stood for a moment as if looking after the visionary passenger. "We are not afraid," she said, "even the youngest; we all know she is our friend."

When we had got back to the side of the loch, where, I confess, I was pleased to find myself, in the free open air without any perplexing shadow of trees, I felt less objection to the subject. "I wish you would tell me the story; for of course there is a story?" I said.

"No, there is no story—at least nothing tragical or even romantic. They say she was the eldest daughter. I sometimes wonder," Chatty said, with a smile and a faint increase of colour, "whether she might not be a little like me. She lived here all her life, and had several generations to take care of. Oh no, there was no murder or wrong about our Lady; she just loved Ellermore above everything; and my idea is that she has been allowed the care of us ever since."

"That is very sweet, to have the care of you," I said, scarcely venturing to put any emphasis on the pronoun; "but, after all, it must be slow work, don't you think, walking up and down there for ever? I call that a poor sort of reward for a good woman. If she had been a bad one, it might have answered very well for a punishment."

"Mr. Temple!" Chatty said, now reddening with indignation, "do you think it is a poor thing to have the care of your own people, to watch over them, whatever may happen—to be all for them and their service? I don't think so; I should like to have such a fate."

Perhaps I had spoken thus on purpose to bring about the discussion. "There is such a thing as being too devoted to a family. Are they ever grateful? They go away and marry and leave you in the lurch."

She looked up at me with a little astonishment. "The members may vary, but the family never goes away," she said; "besides, that can apply to us in our present situation only. *She* must have seen so many come and go; but that need not vex her, you know, because they go where she is."

"My dear Miss Campbell, wait a bit; think a little," I said. "Where she is! That is in the Lady's Walk, according to your story. Let us hope that all your ancestors and relations are not there."

"I suppose you want to make me angry," said Chatty. "She is in heaven—have you any doubt of that?—but every day when the sun is setting she comes back home."

"Oh, come!" I said, "if it is only at the sunset, that is not so bad."

Miss Campbell looked at me doubtfully, as if not knowing whether to be angry. "You want to make fun of it," she said, "to laugh at it; and yet," she added, with a little spirit, "you were very nervous half an hour ago."

"I acknowledge to being nervous. I am very impressionable. I believe that is the word. It is a luxury like another to be nervous at the fit moment. Frightened, you might say, if you prefer plain speaking. And I am very glad it is at sunset, not in the dark. This completes the circle of my Highland experiences," I said; "everything now is perfect. I have shot grouse on the hill and caught trout on the loch, and been soaked to the skin and then dried in the wind; I wanted nothing but the family ghost. And now I have seen her, or at least heard her" —

"If you are resolved to make a joke of it I cannot help it," said Chatty, "but I warn you that it is not agreeable to me, Mr. Temple. Let us talk of something else. In the Highlands," she said, with dignity, "we take different views of many things."

"There are some things," I said, "of which but one view is possible — that I should have the audacity and impertinence to laugh at anything for which you have a veneration! I believe it is only because I was so frightened" —

She smiled again in her lovely motherly way, a smile of indulgence and forgiveness and bounty. "You are too humble now," she said, "and I think I hear someone calling me. It is time to go in."

And to be sure there was someone calling her; there always was, I think, at all hours of the night and day.

CHAPTER II

TO say that I got rid of the recollection of the Lady of Ellermore when I went upstairs, after a cheerful evening, through a long and slippery gallery to my room in the wing, would be untrue. The curious experience I had just had dwelt in my mind with a touch of not unpleasant perplexity. "Of course," I said to myself, "there must be something to account for those footsteps—some hidden way in which the sounds must come." Perhaps my first idea would turn out to be correct—that there was a byroad to the farm or to the stables, which in some states of the atmosphere, or perhaps it might even be always, echoed back the sounds of passing feet in some subterranean vibration. One has heard of such things, one has heard, indeed, of every kind of natural wonder, some of them no more easy to explain than the other interpretation; but so long as you have science with you, whether you understand it or not, you are all right. I could not help wondering, however, whether, if by chance I heard those steps in the long gallery outside my door, I should refer the matter comfortably to the science of acoustics. I was tormented, until I fell asleep, by a vague expectation of hearing them. I could not get them out of my mind or out of my ears, so distinct were they—the light step, soft but with energy in it, evidently a woman's step. I could not help recollecting, with a tingling sensation through all my veins, the distinctness of the turn it gave—the coming back, the steps going in a line opposite to ours. It seemed to me that from moment to moment I must hear it again in the gallery, and then how could it be explained?

Next day—for I slept very well after I had succeeded in getting to sleep, and what I had heard did not by any means haunt my dreams—next day I managed to elude all the pleasant occupations of the house, and, as soon as I could get free from observation, I took my way to the Lady's Walk. I had said that I had letters to write—a well-worn phrase, which of course means exactly what one pleases. I walked up and down the Lady's Walk, and could neither hear nor see anything. On this side of the shrubbery there was no possibility of any concealed path; on the other side the bank went sloping to the water's edge. The avenue ran along from the corner of the loch half-way round the green plateau on which the house was planted, and at the upper end came out upon the elevated ground behind the house; but no road crossed it, nor was there the slightest appearance of any mode by which a steady sound not its own could be communicated here. I examined it all with the utmost care, looking behind the bole of every tree, as if the secret might be there, and my heart gave a leap when I perceived what seemed to me one narrow track worn along the ground. Fancy plays us curious pranks even when she is most on her guard. It was a strange idea that I, who had come here with the purpose of finding a way of explaining the curious phenomena upon which so long and lasting a superstition had been built, should be so quickly infected by it. I saw the little track, quite narrow but very distinct, and though of course I did not believe in the Lady of Ellermore, yet within myself I jumped at the certainty that this was her track. It gave me a curious sensation. The certainty lay underneath the scepticism, as if they were two things which had no connection with each other. Had anyone seen me it must have been supposed that I was looking for something among the bushes, so closely did I scrutinise every foot of the soil and every tree.

It exercised a fascination upon me which I could not resist. The Psychical Society did not exist in those days, so far as I know, but there are many minds outside that inquisitive body to whom the authentication of a ghost story, or, to speak more practically, the clearing up of a superstition, is very attractive. I managed to elude the family arrangements once more at the same hour at which Miss Campbell and I had visited the Lady's Walk on the previous evening. It was a lovely evening, soft and warm, the western sky all ablaze with colour, the great branches of the beeches thrown out in dark maturity of greenness upon the flush of orange and crimson, melting into celestial rosy red as it rose higher, and flinging itself in frothy heaps across the serene blue above. The same wonderful colours glowed in reflection out of the loch. The air was of magical clearness, and earth and sky seemed stilled with an almost awe of their own loveliness, happiness, and peace.

> "The holy time was quiet as a nun,
> Breathless with adoration."

For my part, however, I noticed this only in passing, being intent on other thoughts. From the loch there came a soft tumult of voices. It was Saturday evening, and all the boys were at home. They were getting out the boats for an evening row, and the white sail of the toy yacht rose upon the gleaming water like a little white cloud among the rosy clouds of that resplendent sky. I stood between two of the beeches that formed a sort of arch, and looked out upon them, distracted for an instant by the pleasant distant sound which came softly through the summer air. Next moment I turned sharply round with a start, in spite of myself; turned quickly to see who it was coming after me. There was, I need not say, not a soul within sight. The beeches fluttered softly in the warm air; the long shadows of their great boles lay unbroken along the path; nothing else was visible, not even a bird on a bank. I stood breathless between the two trees, with my back turned to the loch, gazing at nothing, while the soft footsteps came quietly on, and passed me—passed me! with a slight waft of air, I thought, such as a slight, light figure might have made; but that was imagination perhaps. Imagination! was it not all imagination? or what was it? No shadows or darkness to conceal a form by; full light of day radiant with colour; the most living, delightful air, all sweet with pleasure. I stood there speechless and without power to move. *She* went along softly, without changing the gentle regularity of her tread, to the end of the walk. The steps grew fainter as they went farther and farther from me. I never listened so intently in my life. I said to myself, "If they go out of hearing I shall know it is merely an excited imagination." And on they went, almost out of hearing, only the faintest touch upon the ground; then there was a momentary pause, and my heart stood still, but leaped again to my throat and sent wild waves of throbbing to my ears next moment: they had turned and were coming back.

I cannot describe the extraordinary effect. If it had been dark it would have been altogether different. The brightness, the life around, the absence of all that one associates with the supernatural, produced a thrill of emotion to which I can give no name. It was not fear; yet my heart beat as it had never done in any dangerous emergency (and I have passed through some that were exciting enough) before; my breath seemed to go away from me. Would she come back to where I was? She did, passing me once more, with the same movement of the air (or so I thought), and turned again. But by that time my pulses were all clanging so in my ears that I could bear it no longer. I turned and walked precipitately away, stumbling down the little slope and losing myself in the shrubberies which were beneath the range of the low sun, now almost set, and felt dank and cold in the contrast. It was something like plunging into a bath of cold air after the warmth and glory above.

It was in this way that my first experience ended. Miss Campbell looked at me a little curiously with a half-smile when I joined the party at the loch side. She divined where I had been, and perhaps something of the strange agitation I felt, but she took no further notice; and as I was in time to find a place in the boat, where she had established herself with the children, I lost nothing by my meeting with the mysterious passenger in the Lady's Walk.

I did not go near the place for some days afterwards, but I cannot say that it was ever long out of my thoughts. I had long arguments with myself on the subject, representing to myself that I had heard the sound before hearing the superstition, and then had found no difficulty in believing that it was the sound of some passenger on an adjacent path, perhaps invisible from the walk. I had not been able to find that path, but still it might exist at some angle which, according to the natural law of the transmission of sounds—Bah! what jargon this was! Had I not heard *her* turn, felt her pass me, watched her coming back? And then I paused with a loud burst of laughter at myself. "Ass! you never had any of these sensations before you heard the story," I said. And that was true; but I heard the steps before I heard the story; and, now I think of it, was much startled by them, and set my mind to work to account for them, as you know. "And what evidence have you that the first interpretation was not the right one?" myself asked me with scorn; upon which question I turned my back with a hopeless contempt of the pertinacity of that other person who has always so many objections to make. Interpretation! could any interpretation ever do away with the effect upon my actual senses of that invisible passer-by? But the most disagreeable effect was this, that I could not shut out from my mind the expectation of hearing those same steps in the gallery outside my door at night. It was a long gallery, running the full length of the wing, highly polished and somewhat slippery, a place in which any sound was important. I never went along to my room without a feeling that at any moment I might hear those steps behind me, or after I had closed my door might be conscious of them passing. I never did so, but neither have I ever got free of the thought.

A few days after, however, another incident occurred that drove the Lady's Walk and its invisible visitor out of my mind. We were all returning home in the long northern twilight from a mountain expedition. How it was that I was the last to return I do not exactly recollect. I think Miss Campbell had forgotten to give some directions to the watchman's wife at the lodge, which I volunteered to carry for her. My nearest way back would have been through the Lady's Walk, had not some sort of doubtful feeling restrained me from taking it. Though I have said and felt that the effect of these mysterious footsteps was enhanced by the full daylight, still I had a sort of natural reluctance to put myself in the way of encountering them when the darkness began to fall. I preferred the shrubberies, though they were darker and less attractive. As I came out of their shade, however, someone met me, coming apparently from that direction. I thought at first it was Charlotte, for the outline was like hers. It was almost dark, and what little light there was was behind her, so that I could not distinguish her features. She was tall and slight, and wrapped apparently in a long cloak, a dress usual enough in those rainy regions. I think, too, that her veil was over her face. The way in which she approached made it apparent that she was going to speak to me, which surprised me a little, though there was nothing extraordinary in it; for of course by this time all the neighbourhood knew who I was and that

I was a visitor at Ellermore. There was a little air of timidity and hesitation about her as she came forward, from which I supposed that my sudden appearance startled her a little, and yet was welcome as an unexpected way of getting something done that she wanted. *Tant de choses en un mot*, you will say—and yet it was quite true. She came up to me quickly as soon as she had made up her mind. Her voice was very soft, but very peculiar, with a sort of far-away sound, as if the veil or evening air interposed a sort of visionary distance between her and me. "I cannot speak to them. I must not speak to them," she said, then paused a little and seemed to look at me with eyes that shone dimly through the shadows like stars in a misty sky.

"Can I be of any use to you? I am living here," I said, very much surprised.

"Tell them it's Colin! Colin! in trouble and temptation. Oh, and I must not speak!"

"Colin!" I said, startled; then, after a moment, "Pardon me, this is an uncomfortable message to entrust to a stranger. Is he ill? What must I tell them?" I was still less interested than surprised.

"In great trouble and temptation," she repeated, with a sort of wail. "Oh, the bonnie boy, the bonnie boy!"

"Stop," I cried, "stop!" for she seemed about to pass on. "If I am to say this there must be something more. Who is it that sends the message? They will ask me, of course. And what is wrong?"

She seemed to wring her hands under her cloak, and looked at me with an attitude and gesture of supplication. "In great trouble," she said, "in great trouble! And me, I can do nothing; nor even speak, nor even speak!"

And, notwithstanding all that I could say, she left me so, with a wave of her hand, disappearing among the dark bushes. It may be supposed that this was no agreeable charge to give to a guest, one who owed nothing but pleasure and kindness to the Campbells, but had no acquaintance beyond the surface with their concerns. They were, it is true, very free in spirit, and seemed to have as little *dessous des cartes* in their life and affairs as could be imagined. But Colin was the one who was spoken of less freely than any other in the family. He had been expected several times since I came, but had never appeared. It seemed that he had a way of postponing his arrival, and "of course," it was said in the family, never came when he was expected. I had wondered more than once at the testy tone in which the old gentleman spoke of him sometimes, and the line of covert defence always adopted by Charlotte. To be sure, he was the eldest, and might naturally assume a greater independence of action than the other young men, who were yet scarcely beyond the age of pupilage and in their father's house.

But from this, as well as from the still more natural and apparent reason that to bring them bad news of any kind was most disagreeable and inappropriate on my part, the commission I had so strangely received hung very heavily upon me. I turned it over in my mind as I dressed for dinner (we had been out all day, and dinner was much later than usual in consequence) with great perplexity and distress. Was I bound to give a message forced upon me in such a way? If the lady had news of any importance to give, why did she turn away from the house, where she could have communicated it at once, and confide it to a stranger? On the other hand, would I be justified in keeping back anything that might be of so much importance to them? It might perhaps be something for which she did not wish to give her authority. Sometimes people in such circumstances will even condescend to write an anonymous letter to give the warning they think necessary, without betraying to the victims of misfortune that anyone whom they know is acquainted with it. Here was a justification for the strange step she had taken. It might be done in the utmost kindness to them, if not to me; and what if there might be some real danger afloat and Colin be in peril, as she said? I thought over these things anxiously before I went downstairs, but even up to the moment of entering that bright and genial drawing-room, so full of animated faces and cheerful talk, I had not made up my mind what I should do. When we returned to it after dinner I was still uncertain. It was late, and the children were sent to bed. The boys went round to the stables to see that the horses were not the worse for their day's work. Mr. Campbell retired to his library. For a little while I was left alone, a thing that very rarely happened. Presently Miss Campbell came downstairs from the children's rooms, with that air about her of rest and sweetness, like a reflection of the little prayers she has been hearing and the infant repose which she has left, which hangs about a young mother when she has disposed her babies to sleep. Charlotte, by her right of being no mother, but only a voluntary mother by deputy, had a still more tender light about her in the sweetness of this duty which God and her goodwill, not simple nature, had put upon her. She came softly into the room with her shining countenance. "Are you alone, Mr. Temple?" she said, with a little surprise. "How rude of those boys to leave you," and came and drew her chair towards the table where I was in the kindness of her heart.

"I am very glad they have left me if I may have a little talk with you," I said; and then, before I knew, I had told her. She was the kind of woman to whom it is a relief to tell whatever may be on your heart. The fact that it was her own concern seemed to move her less than the care to myself. She was very much surprised and disturbed. "Colin in trouble? Oh, that might very well be," she said, then stopped herself. "You are his friend," she said; "you will not misunderstand me, Mr. Temple. He is very independent, and not so open as the rest of us. That is nothing against him. We are all rather given to talking; we keep nothing to ourselves—except Colin. And then he is more away than the rest." The first necessity in her mind seemed to be this, of defending the absent. Then came the question, From whom could the warning be? Charley came in at this moment, and she called him to her eagerly. "Here is a very strange thing happened. Somebody came up to Mr. Temple in the shrubbery and told him to tell us that Colin was in trouble."

"Colin!" I could see that Charley was, as Charlotte had been, more distressed than surprised. "When did you hear from him last?" he said.

"On Monday; but the strange thing is, who could it be that sent such a message? You said a lady, Mr. Temple?"

"What like was she?" said Charley.

Then I described as well as I could. "She was tall and very slight; wrapped up in a cloak, so that I could not make out much, and her veil down. And it was almost dark."

"It is clear she did not want to be recognised," Charley said.

"There was something peculiar about her voice, but I really cannot describe it; a strange tone, unlike anything" —

"Marion Gray has a peculiar voice; she is tall and slight. But what could she know about Colin?"

"I will tell you who is more likely," cried Charley, "and that is Susie Cameron. Her brother is in London now; they may have heard from him."

"Oh, Heaven forbid! oh, Heaven forbid! the Camerons of all people!" Charlotte cried, wringing her hands. The action struck me as so like that of the veiled stranger that it gave me a curious shock. I had not time to follow out the vague, strange suggestion that it seemed to breathe into my mind; but the sensation was as if I had suddenly, groping, come upon someone in the dark.

"Whoever it was," I said, "she was not indifferent, but full of concern and interest" —

"Susie would be that," Charley said, looking significantly at his sister, who rose from her chair in great distress.

"I would telegraph to him at once," she said, "but it is too late to-night."

"And what good would it do to telegraph? If he is in trouble it would be no help to him."

"But what can I do? what else can I do?" she cried. I had plunged them into sudden misery, and could only look on now as an anxious but helpless spectator, feeling at the same time as if I had intruded myself upon a family affliction; for it was evident that they were not at all unprepared for "trouble" to Colin. I felt my position very embarrassing, and rose to go away.

"I feel miserably guilty," I said, "as if I had been the bearer of bad news; but I am sure you will believe that I would not for anything in the world intrude upon" —

Charlotte paused to give me a pale sort of smile, and pointed to the chair I had left. "No, no," she said, "don't go away, Mr. Temple. We do not conceal from you that we are anxious—that we were anxious even before—but don't go away. I don't think I will tell my father, Charley. It would break his rest. Let him have his night's rest whatever happens, and there is nothing to be done to-night" —

"We will see what the post brings to-morrow," Charley said.

And then the consultation ended abruptly by the sudden entrance of the boys, bringing a gust of fresh night air with them. The horses were not a grain the worse, though they had been out all day; even old Grumbling Geordie, the coachman, had not a word to say. "You may have them again to-morrow, Chatty, if you like," said Tom. She had sat down to her work, and met their eyes with an unruffled countenance. "I hope I am not so unreasonable," she said, with her tranquil looks; only I could see a little tremor in her hand, as she stooped over the socks she was knitting. She laid down her work after a while, and went to the piano and played accompaniments, to which first Jack and then Tom sang. She did it without any appearance of effort, yielding to all the wishes of the youngsters, while I looked on wondering. How can women do this sort of thing? It is more than one can divine.

Next morning Mr. Campbell asked "by the bye," but with a pucker in his forehead, which, being now enlightened on the subject, I could understand, if there was any letter from Colin. "No," Charlotte said (who, for her part, had turned over all her letters with a swift, anxious scrutiny). "But that is nothing," she said, "for we heard on Monday." The old gentleman uttered a "Umph!" of displeasure. "Tell him I think it a great want in manners that he is not here to receive Mr. Temple." "Oh, father, Mr. Temple understands," cried Charlotte, and she turned upon me those mild eyes, in which there was now a look that went to my heart, an appeal at once to my sympathy and my forbearance, bidding me not to ask, not to speak, yet to feel with her all the same. If she could have known the rush of answering feeling with which my heart replied; but I had to be careful not even to *look* too much knowledge, too much sympathy.

After this two days passed without any incident. What letters were sent, or other communications, to Colin I could not tell. They were great people for the telegraph, and flashed messages about continually. There was a telegraph station in the little village, which had been very surprising to me at first; but I no longer wondered, seeing their perpetual use of it. People who have to do with business, with great "works" to manage, get into the way more easily than we others. But either no answer or nothing of a satisfactory character was obtained, for I was told no more. The second evening was Sunday, and I was returning alone from a ramble down the glen. It was Mr. Campbell's custom to read a sermon on Sunday evenings to his household, and as I had, in conformity to the custom of the family, already heard two at church, I had deserted on this occasion, and chosen the freedom and quiet of a rural walk instead. It was a cloudy evening, and there had been rain. The clouds hung low on the hills, and half the surrounding peaks had retired altogether into the mist. I had scarcely set foot within the gates when I met once more the lady whose message had brought so much pain. The trees arched over the approach at this spot, and even in full daylight it was in deep shade. Now in the evening dimness it was dark as night. I could see little more than the slim, straight figure, the sudden perception of which gave me—I could scarcely tell why—a curious thrill of something like fear. She came hurriedly towards me, an outline, nothing more, until the same peculiar voice, sweet but sharp, broke the silence. "Did you tell them?" she said.

It cost me an effort to reply calmly. My heart had begun to beat with an excitement over which I had no control, like a horse that takes fright at something which its rider cannot see. I said, "Yes, I told them," straining my eyes, yet feeling as if my faculties were restive like that same horse, and would not obey me, would not look or examine her appearance as I desired. But indeed it would have been in vain, for it was too dark to see.

"But there's nothing done, nothing done!" she said. "Would I come for nothing?" And there was again that movement, the same as I had seen in Charlotte, of wringing her hands.

"Pardon me," I said, "will you tell me who you are? I am a stranger here; no doubt if you would see Miss Campbell herself, or tell me who it is"—

I felt the words somehow arrested in my throat, and she drew back from me with a sudden movement. It is hard to characterise a gesture in the dark, but there seemed to be a motion of impatience and despair in it. "Who would I be?" she cried, "that could not speak? It's because you're a stranger, and wish them well. Colin, Colin! oh, the bonnie boy!"

"I will carry your message, but, for God's sake, if it is so important, tell me who sends it," I said.

She shook her head and went rapidly past me, notwithstanding the anxious appeals that I tried to make. She seemed to put out a hand to wave me back as I stood gazing after her. Just then the lodge door opened. I suppose the woman within had been disturbed by the sound of the voices, and a gleam of firelight burst out upon the road. Across this gleam I saw the slight figure pass quickly, and then a capacious form with a white apron came out and stood in the door. The sight of the coachman's wife in her large and comfortable proportions gave me a certain ease, I cannot tell why. I hurried up to her. "Who was that that passed just now?" I asked.

"That passed just now? There was naebody passed. I thought I heard a voice, and that it was maybe Geordie; but nobody has passed here that I could see."

"Nonsense! you must have seen her," I cried hastily; "she cannot be out of sight yet. No doubt you would know who she was—a lady, tall and slight—in a cloak" —

"Eh, sir, ye maun be joking!" cried the woman. "What lady, if it werna Miss Chatty, would be walking here at this time of the night? Lady! it might maybe be the schoolmaster's daughter. She has one of those ulsters like her betters. But naebody has passed here this hour back, o' that I'm confident," she said.

"Why did you come out, then, just at this moment?" I cried. The woman contemplated me in the gleam from the fire from top to toe. "You're the English gentleman that's biding up at the house," she said. "'Deed, I just heard a step, that was nae doubt your step, and I thought it might be my man; but there has naebody, far less a lady, whatever she had on, passed my door coming or going. Is that you, Geordie?" she cried suddenly, as a step became audible approaching the gate from the outer side.

"Ay, it's just me," responded her husband out of the gloom.

"Have ye met a leddy as ye came along? The gentleman here will have it that there's been a leddy passing the gate, and there's been no leddy. I would have seen her through the window even if I hadna opened the door."

"I've seen no leddy," said Geordie, letting himself in with considerable noise at the foot entrance, which I now remembered to have closed behind me when I passed through it a few minutes before. "I've met no person; it's no' an hour for leddies to be about the roads on Sabbath day at e'en."

It was at this moment that a wild suggestion darted into my mind. How it came I cannot tell. I was not the sort of man, I said to myself, for any such folly. My imagination had been a little touched, to be sure, by that curious affair of the footsteps; but this, which seemed to make my heart stand still and sent a shiver through me, was very different, and it was a folly not to be entertained for a moment. I stamped my foot upon it instantly, crushing it on the threshold of the mind. "Apparently either you or I must be mistaken," I said, with a laugh at the high tone of Geordie, who himself had evidently been employed in a jovial way—quite consistent, according to all I had heard, with very fine principles in respect to the Sabbath. I had a laugh over this as I went away, insisting upon the joke to myself as I hurried up the avenue. It was extremely funny, I said to myself; it would be a capital story among my other Scotch experiences. But somehow my laugh died away in a very feeble sort of quaver. The night had grown dark even when I emerged from under the trees, by reason of a great cloud, full of rain, which had rolled up over the sky, quenching it out. I was very glad to see the lights of the house gleaming steadily before me. The blind had not been drawn over the end window of the drawing-room, and from the darkness without I looked in upon a scene which was full of warmth and household calm. Though it was August there was a little glimmer of fire. The reading of the sermon was over. Old Mr. Campbell still sat at a little table with the book before him, but it was closed. Charlotte in the foreground, with little Harry and Mary on either side of her, was "hearing their paraphrase." [A]

The boys were putting a clever dog through his tricks in a sort of clandestine way behind backs, at whom Charlotte would shake a finger now and then with an admonitory smiling look. Charley was reading or writing at the end of the room. The soft little chime of the children's voices, the suppressed laughter and whispering of the boys, the father's leisurely remark now and then, made up a soft murmur of sound which was like the very breath of quietude and peace. How did I dare, their favoured guest, indebted so deeply as I was to their kindness, to go in among them with that mysterious message and disturb their tranquillity once more?

When I went into the drawing-room, which was not till an hour later, Charlotte looked up at me smiling, with some playful remark as to my flight from the evening reading. But as she caught my eye her countenance changed. She put down her book, and after a little consideration walked to that end window through which I had looked, and which was in a deep recess, making me a little sign to follow her. "How dark the night is," she said, with a little pretence of looking out, and then in a hurried under-tone, "Mr. Temple, you have heard something more?"

"Not any more, but certainly the same thing repeated. I have seen the lady again."

"And who is she? Tell me frankly, Mr. Temple. Just the same thing—that Colin is in trouble? no details? I cannot imagine who can take so much interest. But you asked her for her name?"

"I asked her, but she gave me no reply. She waved her hand and went on. I begged her to see you, and not to give me such a commission; but it was of no use. I don't know if I ought to trouble you with a vague warning that only seems intended to give pain."

"Oh yes," she cried, "oh yes, it was right to tell me. If I only knew who it was! Perhaps you can describe her better, since you have seen her a second time. But Colin has friends—whom we don't know. Oh, Mr. Temple, it is making a great claim upon your kindness, but could not you have followed her and found out who she was?"

"I might have done that," I said. "To tell the truth, it was so instantaneous and I was so startled."

She looked up at me quickly with a questioning air, and grew a little pale, gazing at me; but whether she comprehended the strange wild fancy which I could not even permit myself to realise I cannot tell; for Charley, seeing us standing together, and being in a state of nervous anxiety, also here came and joined us, and we stood talking together in an undertone till Mr. Campbell called to know if anything was the matter. "You are laying your heads together like a set of conspirators," said the old gentleman, with a half-laugh. His manner to me was always benign and gracious; but now that I knew something of the family troubles, I could perceive a vein of suppressed irritation, a certain watchfulness, which made him alarming to the other members of the household. Charlotte gave us both a warning look. "I will tell him to-morrow—I will delay no longer—but not to-night," she said. "Mr. Temple was telling us about his ramble, father. He has just come in in time to avoid the rain."

"Well," said the old man, "he cannot expect to be free from rain up here in the Highlands. It is wonderful the weather we have had." And with this the conversation fell into a very domestic channel. Miss Campbell this time could not put away the look of excitement and agitation in her eyes. But she escaped with the children to see them put to bed, and we sat and talked of politics and other mundane subjects. The boys were all going to leave

Ellermore next day—Tom and Jack for the "works," Charley upon some other business. Mr. Campbell made me formal apologies for them. "I had hoped Colin would have been at home before now to do the honours of the Highlands; but we expect him daily," he said. He kept his eye fixed upon me as if to give emphasis to his words and defy any doubt that might arise in my mind.

Next morning I was summoned by Charley before I came downstairs to "come quickly and speak to my father." I found him in the library, which opened from the dining-room. He was walking about the room in great agitation. He began to address me almost before I was in sight.

"Who is this, sir, that you have been having meetings with about Colin? Some gossip or other that has taken ye in. I need not tell you, Mr. Temple, a lawyer and an Englishman, that an anonymous statement"—For once the old gentleman had forgotten himself, his respect for his guest, his fine manners. He was irritated, obstinate, wounded in pride and feeling. Charlotte touched him on the arm with a murmured appeal, and turned her eyes to me in anxious deprecation. But there was no thought farther from my mind than that of taking offence.

"I fully feel it," I said; "nor was it my part to bring any disagreeable suggestions into this house—if it had not been that my own mind was so burdened with it and Miss Campbell so clear-sighted."

He cast a look at her, half affectionate, half displeased, and then he said to me testily, "But who was the woman? That is the question; that is what I want to know."

My eyes met Charlotte's as I looked up. She had grown very pale, and was gazing at me eagerly, as if she had divined somehow the wild fancy which once more shot across my mind against all reason and without any volition of mine.

CHAPTER III

MR. CAMPBELL was not to be moved. He was very anxious, angry, and ill at ease; but whether it was that he would not betray to me that the message, which he viewed as an anonymous statement, could cause him any uneasiness, or whether it was perplexity and confusion of mind, or if he really felt a confidence which neither his son nor daughter shared, I cannot tell. But he refused to be influenced in any way by this strange communication. It would be some intrusive woman, he said; some busybody—there were many about—who, thinking she could escape being found out in that way, had thought it a grand opportunity of making mischief. He made me a great many apologies for his first hasty words. It was very ill-bred, he said; he was ashamed to think that he had let himself be so carried away; but he would hear nothing of the message itself. It appeared that Miss Campbell had both written and telegraphed to her brother. To the letter there was as yet no reply; but Colin had answered the telegram by a somewhat angry one, declaring that he was all right. "What more would you have him to do?" Mr. Campbell said, with a sort of restrained fury. Charlotte said nothing more in my presence, but I divined that she was anxiously endeavouring to induce him, if not to go himself, yet to permit her to go to her brother. The position was a very embarrassing one, especially when all the brothers left for their business, which they did by the morning boat. It seemed out of all character that a stranger should remain in the circumstances; so I contrived to have a letter by the midday post summoning me back to town. They were, of course, quite well aware that letters do not come from London on a Monday; but Charlotte at least made no remark. Her father looked at me rather fiercely, being irritated and susceptible, and disposed to take offence at anything that seemed to attach importance to this curious episode; and the children made a great outcry and lamentation; but they did not make any serious attempt to change my resolution. It was even agreeable to Miss Campbell I saw, and this gave me a pang, anxious as I was to be agreeable to her in every way. The last boat would get me to the nearest station in time for the night train, or it was suggested that I might be driven there, which would give me still more time. I had made all my arrangements, and had come downstairs again, somewhat forlorn, to have my last talk with the woman whose sweet company during these two or three weeks past had been more to me than I could say. I found her with her hat on, waiting for me in the hall. "I thought you would like to take one turn more," she said, with a smile, in which (I hoped) there was some sadness. There was certainly excitement in her eyes, in her movements a sort of eagerness and almost impatience. We went out and walked across the lawn to the side of the loch. The sun was beginning to sink; the sky was all aglow, putting on by degrees the gorgeous hues of a northern sunset. She said nothing till we were clear of all possibility of listeners—too far off for the children to rush out upon us, as they so often did. Then she paused suddenly, and looked up into my face. "Mr. Temple," she said, "you will think me heartless, letting you go without a word, though well I know the reason why. You think you are a trouble to us at such a time. Oh no, you are no trouble. But I am selfish; I don't wish to detain you—I want you to do something for me."

"Anything," I cried, "anything—whatever man can."

"I knew you would say so; that is why I have scarcely said I am sorry. I have not tried to stop you. Mr. Temple, I am not shutting my eyes to it like my father. I am sure that, whoever it was that spoke to you, the warning was true. I want you to go to Colin," she said abruptly, after a momentary pause, "and let me know the truth."

"To Colin?" I cried. "But you know how little acquainted we are. It was not he who wrote to me, but Charley"—

"And I. You don't leave me out, I hope," she said, with a faint smile. "But what could make a better excuse than that you have been here? Mr. Temple, you will go when I ask you? Oh, I do more—I entreat you! Go, and let me know the truth."

"Of course I shall go—from the moment you ask me, Miss Campbell; but what if I offend, and make him angry? He may think me a spy upon him. He may think"—

"Oh, Mr. Temple, never mind. You have been so friendly to us. Think what a comfort it will be to me. You have been mixed up in it all. You are not like a stranger; and yet if you knew the comfort, the satisfaction it is that you *are* a stranger! Do you know what I mean? I can speak to you. It is not like exposing my poor Colin to somebody who has known him all his life, and who will say, 'I knew this was what would happen.' Do you know what I mean?" she asked, with the tears in her eyes.

And I hope I was man enough to understand without either offence or thinking too much of the confidence thus given to me. I perceived that I was a sort of forlorn hope; that I was like a rope thrown out to a drowning man; all the more prized because I was not of them—perhaps because I would disappear—my use being served—and be seen no more. But this was not—oh, surely not—what she meant! She was not a woman to throw anyone over who had served her. We walked up and down the side of the water, which every moment grew more and more into a blazing mirror, a burnished shield decked with every imaginable colour, though our minds had no room for its beauty, and it only touched my eyesight in coming and going. There she told me much about Colin, which I had not known or guessed—about his inclinations and tastes, which were not like any of the others, and how his friends and his ways were unknown to them. "But we have always hoped this would pass away," she said, "for his heart is good; oh, his heart is good! You remember how kind he was to me when we met you first? He is always kind." Thus we walked and talked until I had seen a new side at once of her character and life. The home had seemed to me so happy and free from care; but the dark shadow was there as everywhere, and her heart often wrung with suspense and anguish. We then returned slowly towards the house, still absorbed in this conversation, for it was time that I should go in and eat my last meal at Ellermore.

We had come within sight of the door, which stood open as always, when we suddenly caught sight of Mr. Campbell posting towards us with a wild haste, so unlike his usual circumspect walk that I was startled. His feet seemed to twist as they sped along, in such haste was he. His hat was pushed back on his head, his coat-tails flying behind him—precipitate, like a man pursued, or in one of those panics which take away breath and sense, or, still more perhaps, as if a strong wind were behind him, blowing him on. When he came within speech of us, he called out hurriedly, "Come here! come here, both of you!" and turning, hastened back with the same breathless hurry, beckoning with his hand. "He must have heard something more," Charlotte said, and rushed after him. I followed a few steps behind. Mr. Campbell said nothing to his daughter when she made up to him. He almost pushed her off when she put her hand through his arm. He had no leisure even for sympathy. He hurried along with feet that stumbled in sheer haste till he came to the Lady's Walk, which lay in the level sunshine, a path of gold between the great boles of the trees. It was a slight ascent, which tried him still more. He went a few yards along the path, then stopped and looked round upon her and me, with his hand raised to call our attention. His face was perfectly colourless. Alarm and dismay were written on every line of it. Large drops of perspiration stood upon his forehead. He seemed to desire to speak, but could not; then held up his finger to command our attention. For the first moment or two my attention was so concentrated upon the man and the singularity of his look and gesture, that I thought of nothing else. What did he want us to do? We stood all three in the red light, which seemed to send a flaming sword through us. There was a faint stir of wind among the branches overhead, and a twitter of birds; but in the great stillness the faint lap of the water upon the shore was audible, though the loch was at some distance. Great stillness—that was the word; there was nothing moving but these soft actions of nature. Ah! this was what it was! Charlotte grew perfectly pale too, like her father, as she stood and listened. I seem to see them now: the old man with his white head, his ghastly face, the scared and awful look in his eyes, and she gazing at him, all her faculties involved in the art of listening, her very attitude and drapery listening too, her lips dropping apart, the life ebbing out of her, as if something was draining the blood from her heart.

Mr. Campbell's hand dropped. "She's away," he said, "she's away," in tones of despair; then, with a voice that was shaken by emotion, "I thought it was maybe my fault. By times you say I am getting stupid." There was the most heart-rending tone in this I ever heard—the pained humility of the old confessing a defect, lit up with a gleam of feverish hope that in this case the defect might be a welcome explanation.

"Father dear," cried Charlotte, putting her hand on his arm—she had looked like fainting a moment before, but recovered herself—"it may be only a warning. It may not be desperate even now."

All that the old man answered to this was a mere repetition, pathetic in its simplicity. "She's away, she's away." Then, after a full minute's pause, "You mind when that happened last?" he said.

"Oh, father! oh, father!" cried Charlotte. I withdrew a step or two from this scene. What had I, a stranger, to do with it? They had forgotten my presence, and at the sound of my step they both looked up with a wild, eager look in their faces, followed by blank disappointment. Then he sighed, and said, with a return of composure, "You will throw a few things into a bag, and we'll go at once, Chatty. There is no time to lose."

They went down to the house together, arm in arm, and I remained alone in the Lady's Walk. My head was turning round. Was it the most superstitious folly? What was it? Common sense, which will come in at inconvenient moments and drive one into a corner, stalked forth and looked me, with cynical eyes, in the face. Well! were they mad, or idiots, or what was it? I stood still and listened till my sense of the incongruous and absurd was too much for me. The footsteps which I had once heard so clearly going along this way, and which had in my hearing turned and gone back, were no longer audible. The wind in the branches, the stir of a bird on the bough, the blackbirds singing clear and high in the shrubberies, even, as I have said, the lap of the water on the shore, were audible, but nothing else. I walked along to the end and back again. There was not a sound. Well, I said to myself, I suppose the sound that caused it must be stilled for some reason or other; and I laughed. But next moment I felt the skin creep upon me, a sort of cold shiver rising under the roots of my hair. I was too much, I suppose, under the influence of the family to regard it in a robust and sensible way. Certain it is, that however the science of acoustics might account for it, as a matter of fact those mysterious sounds had ceased and could be heard no more.

The next hour was to me so confused and incoherent that I could make nothing of it. I was left alone. Only a servant came to tell me that the carriage would be at the door at a certain time. Both Charlotte and her father had disappeared, and whether they were going with me, or meant to let me depart without further notice, I could not tell. When the carriage drove to the door, however, they both appeared. Mr. Campbell was carefully wrapped up, though the evening was not cold. He looked more feeble than I had supposed him to be, and older; there was a quiver and twitching about his face, and he tottered as he got with difficulty into the carriage. We drove to the station with scarcely a word. "Have you got the bags right, Chatty? Have you a rug for the journey? Are you sure you brought money enough?"

"Yes, father, yes," Charlotte said. He was evidently altogether dependent upon her. She directed me with a look to give him my arm when we arrived at the railway station, and ran to and fro herself, taking the tickets and doing all that was needful.

"Let me do it," I said; "I cannot bear to see you doing such work."

"You are serving me much better as it is," she said. And then came the long journey, swinging through the night with that great clang of movement and vibration of the separated air, which seems to deafen the mind as well as the body and crush down anxious thought. Mr. Campbell slept a little, with his fine white head relieved against the cushions, and then Charlotte came closer to me and talked. I asked her instructions humbly as to what I should do, and she begged me, with a certain terror in her face, to stay with them, to go with them to Colin's lodgings. She talked a great deal to me in soft tones during the night, with a confidence and familiarity that touched me deeply. It seemed to help her to get through the dreary hours. She told me that it was when her mother died that the steps had been inaudible before. She did not use this phraseology. She said, "When the lady went away before." "Dear Miss Campbell," I said, "you who are so reasonable, so full of sense and thought, what could those sounds have to do with matters so serious? It was a holiday, and the people were away from the farm. No doubt that was the cause. There was no echo from the other road, wherever it may be."

She looked at me with a pitying air. "Do you really believe that?" she said. "And don't you feel the world poor, poor,"—her voice suspended itself a moment on that little national peculiarity, the repetition which gives force—"when, instead of being a good guardian, a kind soul, it is only a vulgar echo, a thing that is nothing?" The water shone in her eyes when she lingered in the slight chant of her speech upon the *good* and *kind*, but dried up and they shone upon me with defiance when she scorned the vulgar, the material. Then she added, with a low voice touched with awe, "And who was it, Mr. Temple, that came to you, that gave you that warning?"

"I have asked myself the question, Miss Campbell."

"Yes, and you have answered it too. Who else? It is that that makes my heart fail," she said.

"If," said I, "we find your brother, as I hope we shall, well and happy"—

Her countenance changed. "In that case—God grant it! oh, God grant it!—you may say what you please, Mr. Temple." Then after a moment she said quickly, "What is that the French say about the unforeseen being always the thing that happens? In that case"—But she did not tell me what it was that she had foreseen.

To have Charlotte there, altogether a thing so far beyond hope, travelling with me, perhaps to owe something to me, and certainly without any doubt to find myself woven in with the web of her life, was so unexpected and so delightful that I could not perhaps be so deeply affected by their troubles as I might have been otherwise. If it was pain to them, it was good to me—I could not but feel the heart rise in my breast, notwithstanding the pathos there was in the old man's feebleness, in the broken sleep into which he fell, and the unprotected openness of his slumbering countenance, all revealed in the pain, the anxiety, the irritation of his misery under the wavering lamp. And yet by moments the pity of it would touch me in spite of myself. An old man, a good man, whose life had been full of kindness done to others—I had seen that and heard of it on all sides. He had given every kind of aid to his dependants. At the "works," to be an orphan was to be the child of the master; and all round him in the country his hand was ever ready—his heart, like his door, always open. And yet this man, who had done so much for others, this was his reward. His own firstborn, the apple of his eye!—I did not know, in so many words, what they feared, but it was not disease or death—it was evil in some shape or other—vice, perhaps crime. God help us all! if justice had been the rule in this world, he must have been defended from every harm by the most spotless, the most devoted of children; his own good deeds would have been returned to him in gratitude and blessing; he would have been the happy man of the Psalms, unashamed in the gates. Alas! and now his grey hairs, his white head was bent low.

We reached London in the fresh early daylight, which made us look all the more fatigued and worn; and then they had a consultation what to do. The decision at last was to postpone for an hour or two the visit to Colin, that Mr. Campbell might get a little rest. I went with them to the hotel. Charlotte said nothing, but she gave me an imploring look, and her father's weakness seemed to grow upon him every hour. He wanted my arm to go upstairs. He looked for me, and called me to his side with a little querulous movement. Perhaps, by some confusion in his mind, he seemed to consider that he had somehow a right to my services. But, though he felt his weakness, he would not suffer Charlotte to go to her brother alone. "I am all right," he said; "I am all right. It is because I have not slept. You young people who sleep, that makes all the difference." He was in reality the only one of us who had slept at all. Breakfast was prepared for us in one of those bare rooms in the great new caravanserai for travellers which are so associated with fatigue and vacancy, with hurried, painful recollections, and melancholy meetings and partings. When I went into it, Charlotte was standing at the window. She called me hastily as soon as I came in. She seized my arm when I came up to her, and drew me close by the window. "Look! was that she?" she cried wildly. "Look! look! or she will be gone." She pointed to the street below, which was alive with a constant succession of passers-by. To make out one from another was difficult enough. They moved and recrossed in front of us, a stream of men and women, never ending. "Is that she?" I looked blankly, now here, now there. "No, no; not that way—to the left," said Charlotte— "there—there!" I saw nothing but a stream of people following and crossing each other, all equally commonplace and unknown. I made her sit down, for she was trembling. "It is impossible," I said, "to distinguish any individual in such a crowded street."

"Oh, not so! not so! I saw her as plainly as I do you now. She was in the midst of a group which seemed to open and let her be seen. She was in a grey cloak and veil, exactly as you described her. She shook her head at me. I almost thought I could hear her speak."

"It is your imagination that is excited. How could you see at that distance, much less hear?"

"I thought," said Charlotte solemnly, "that she said, 'Too late, too late!' I know I could not hear. Do not find fault with me. I am very unhappy. There! there! you can see her now?"

Somebody in a cloak indeed disappeared in the crowd as I looked out, but who it was, how could I tell? Perhaps a workwoman going to her work, or careful manager out to make her market. I took Charlotte's hand, which was trembling, and held it in mine. She was sobbing under her breath. "All this is too much for you," I said. "Find fault with you? Oh that I could take this trouble on my own shoulders, whatever it is!"

She tried to smile as she looked up. "Perhaps," she said, "it was imagination, as you say. What is imagination? Does it make any difference?" She was not aware how much meaning was in her words, but spoke as one bewildered, not knowing what was real and what unreal about her.

It was about eleven o'clock when they set out. I put Mr. Campbell into a cab, where he sat very square, with his staff between his knees, leaning upon it, and his face like that of a benignant old judge, wound up to make a painful decision. Charlotte took her place beside him. For my own part, I sprang into a hansom, and desired the man to follow. It seemed impossible to predict what might happen. I had begun to be superstitious and fanciful myself, and a dozen times over fancied that I saw a woman in a cloak following our course with wistful looks, or shaking her head, as Charlotte had seen her. Had she seen it, or only imagined it? And if the latter, I asked myself in her own words, What difference did it make?

CHAPTER IV

COLIN'S lodgings proved to be in the last place to which I should have thought him likely to have gone—in one of the prim, respectable, old-fashioned streets about Bloomsbury. Probably he felt himself more out of the way of remark there than he would have been in regions more under public inspection, and where acquaintances might have found him more readily. I got out quickly to hand Mr. Campbell from the cab, and he held fast to my arm, apparently with a little confusion of mind. "Yes, I want your arm. I am—a little shaky this morning; don't leave me, Charley!" he said. "Father, it is Mr. Temple," said Charlotte. He looked up at me with dim eyes, and a half smile. "Ay, to be sure, it is Mr. Temple. Never mind, he will just come with me all the same." He had been so determined before not to acknowledge to me any anxiety about Colin, that this sudden abandonment of all reticence struck me with strange surprise. I exchanged a glance with Charlotte over his shoulder. "Will you come, since he says so?" she said. I could not blame her for not wishing for my presence, but I felt by the weight of his hand upon my arm that I was necessary, and said nothing more.

There was evidently a little excitement in the house at the sight of the carriage and the party arriving. The door was opened by a young woman, too much dressed for a servant—the landlady's daughter, no doubt—who came out with the distinct intention of admitting nobody. Yes, Mr. Campbell lived there, she acknowledged; but he was not very well—he was confined to his room. She believed he was still in bed; he had left orders that he could see nobody. "He will see us," said Charlotte. "Will you let us pass at once, please, and show me my brother's room." The young woman gave a little scream. "Oh! I can't let you go in," she cried; "I daren't. What would they all say to me?" "What is all this?" said the old man, pushing forward; indeed, it was I whom he pushed forward, like an implement to clear the way. He made his way thus up the steps and in at the door, the girl retreating before him. This put me forward a little in advance of him into the first room that presented itself, an untidy parlour. Here he resigned my arm and sat down. "Go and tell Colin I am here," he said to his daughter. "Oh! I tell you, Mr. Campbell can't see you—he is ill in bed," cried the girl, shutting the door upon us, and standing with her back to it, evidently too frightened to know what to do. The room was good-sized, though completely out of order, badly furnished and faded. It was connected by folding-doors, which were closed, with another room behind. Presently one of these opened and admitted another young woman, a little older than the first, and still more elaborately dressed, who came into the midst of us with sudden impetuosity, but closed carefully the door behind her. "I would like to know," she said, "who it is that is making so much noise, with a sick person in the house. I am Mrs. Campbell, if you have anything to say to me." She tossed her head with a determined air, confronting Miss Campbell as if this was her natural antagonist. Charlotte gave a low cry. She put herself in her turn before her father, as if to defend him from an encounter so unlooked for. But the old man caught her dress and thrust her out of the way. He rose up tremulous, feeling for my arm. "You are—what?" he said, putting up his hand to his ear.

"Old gentleman," cried the young woman, "I don't know who you are that push in like this to a strange house, nor that person there—that is your daughter, I suppose? If you've got any claim upon him, I'm here to answer for him; he's a gentleman, and we were married at church as good as anybody. If she thinks she has any claim upon him, she's just got to say it to me" —

"Chatty, will this be Colin's wife?"

"It looks like it, father," said Charlotte, with a sorrowful shake of her head. And then she said, "I am very thankful. It might have been worse. If there is no more harm than this, oh, father dear—many a good man has been mistaken. All may be well yet."

"My God! Colin's wife!" the old man cried, pushing me away from him and dropping back into his chair. He had raised his voice, and the words seemed to ring through the house. They were answered by a loud cry and groan mingled together from the other side of the closed door. Then it was pulled open forcibly, and, haggard, unshaven, half-dressed, Colin himself looked in. Never have I seen so tragic a figure. His eyes were bloodshot and wild, his beard half grown, the darkness of his countenance and straggling hair thrown up by the white shirt, crumpled and untidy, which covered his shoulders. He gave one terrible glance round, taking in everything; and I have never myself doubted that, not only the sudden appearance of his father and sister, and the old man's look of death (which none of us perceived at the moment), but the contrast between Charlotte, standing there, and the woman, who immediately began to exclaim at his appearance, and to attempt to force him back again, struck to the very heart of the half-maddened man, and turned the scale at once. He gave one desperate look, pushing off with fury the hand of the wife, which she had laid upon his arm, and disappeared again. The next moment the sharp ring of a pistol shot, close at hand, rang into us all, as if we each had received the bullet. That, I know, was my own sensation. At the same moment there was a heavy fall in the room beyond, and a groan—the only one and the last.

It would be in vain for me to attempt to describe the scene that followed. The woman who had called herself Mrs. Campbell flung open the folding-doors and rushed into the room behind. He was lying in a heap half under a table which had been drawn up to the side of a sofa-bed. He had just risen, it was evident from the tumbled mass of coverings. A cup of tea and the remains of some food were on the table, placed where he could reach them from the bed. He had been at breakfast when this terrible interruption came. On one side of his plate lay a quantity of letters, some of which he had opened. An open case with one pistol in it was on the table. The other lay, with a curl of smoke still about the mouth, on the floor. I followed the woman, who flung herself down beside him on the floor, and made the house resound with her shrieks. I had no special knowledge of such matters, but I had a little experience, and had seen wounds and accidents. I was convinced at the first glance that the doctor, whom I immediately rushed out to seek, was unavailing. The shot had been mortal. But the living had to be cared for, if not the dead. By good fortune I found a doctor only a few doors off, who was still at home, attending to a number of poor patients who crowded about his door. He came with me instantly. I told him what had happened as exactly as I could while we ran from one house to the other. When I took him into the scene of the tragedy, I found the table cleared away, the room open, the morning air from the opened window playing upon the head, heavy as marble, which Charlotte, seated on the floor, was supporting upon her lap. But no one, not even the most inexperienced tyro, would have been deceived in that look. As far from the warm pursuits of the cheerful day as if he had been dead for a century was Colin, never to be called to account for his errors, or shrink from the eye of an angry father in this world any more.

His wife was standing by, crying and scolding together.

"Oh, what did you come here for to drive him wild?" she cried. "He was getting better. And what if he had lost money? there was plenty still. We'd have gone abroad, as he said. We'd have got on. It's not so very much as him and me could have wanted. What did you come here for to madden him altogether? He said as I wasn't to have nothing to do with you. Oh, Campbell! Campbell! can't you hear me crying? It's only a faint. I know it's only a faint. If you would go away and let him be quiet with me, he would come to himself."

The doctor opened the shirt, on which there was scarcely any blood, though it was black with the smoke of the pistol, which seemed to have been placed against it. Charlotte, motionless as the form that leaned upon her, sat with her tearless eyes fixed upon him, following every movement. After a brief examination, the doctor laid his hand gently on her arm.

"If you will let me," he said compassionately, "we will lift him on to the bed." Then he added, still more gently, "You can do nothing more for him."

He and I together, not without difficulty, did this last service. The woman behind broke out into tears and cries, and mingled questions and reproaches.

"It's a faint he is in, doctor. Oh, bring him round, bring him round! What is the good of being a doctor if you cannot do that? It's all their doing, coming so sudden, and he frightened to face them, they're so hard and cruel. Oh, doctor, don't you see he's in a faint? Give him something; do something to bring him to!"

"Try to be quiet," said the doctor, with some severity in his tone. He knew who she was, and thought of her, as was evident, only as the landlady's daughter. "You might take example by this lady, who has far more to do with it. All the doctors in the world could not bring him to, poor fellow! Compose yourself, my good girl, and take the lady away."

The young woman gave a great shriek. "Who are you calling girl?" she cried. "I'm his wife! his lawful wife! and he is only in a faint. Oh, Campbell! Campbell! don't you hear me? Oh, doctor, for God's sake, bring him to!"

Poor creature! beyond her passion and her pride there was some real feeling too. She flung herself at the foot of the bed in a passion of weeping, with loud hysterical shrieks that rang through the house. This brought to her her mother and sister, who, awed by Charlotte's presence, and by the horror of the catastrophe, had been left in the background, but who now rushed in, and, one at either side, began to pour forth mingled wails for the dead and entreaties to the living.

"Take the lady away," the doctor said, turning to me. Charlotte had not moved. She stood at the end of the bed, with a face like marble, not noticing the noise and tumult near her. She might have been all alone with her dead—so still was she; her eyes fixed upon him, the handkerchief in her hand with which she had been bathing his dead forehead. The blow seemed to have struck her to marble. Sometimes her mouth quivered a little, but she did not shed a tear nor utter a word. I took her hand to lead her away, and then she turned a little toward me with a pitiful look.

"We were too late," she said.

"Come away; there is nothing you can do now. Oh, let me take you away; there are others who need you!"

"Nothing I can do," she said dreamily; "nothing anyone can do. Too late! too late!" But she did not move. She was in a region where sounds from without did not reach her. Perhaps, for the moment, it was not even pain she felt, but a wondering awe and solemnity which silenced every thought.

"Charlotte," I cried, being too much moved myself to remember any kind of rule, "where is your father? You have forgotten him! Where has he gone? Your father?" I was alarmed, indeed, at his absence from among the group about poor Colin's bed.

"Ah!" she said, rousing herself with a sigh, that seemed to come from the very bottom of her heart. "My father!" and turned away slowly from the couch and him that lay upon it. The folding-doors were half open, and showed at first only a portion of the chair on which Mr. Campbell had placed himself, and from which it seemed he had never moved. One limp arm and colourless hand hung from the arm of it. His head, sunk upon his breast, was but half visible. For the moment I had no thought but that he had died there, where he sat, and the sight of him added the last horror to the scene. Both dead, father and son, and by one blow!

Charlotte was at his side in a second, while I had done no more than start in my horror. She had loosened the wrappings about his throat, and changed the position of his head, before I could get to her. She was all thought, all energy; she who a moment before had been smitten, too, into marble! Happily, the doctor, who was still there, went to him at once; and we got him laid upon the shabby sofa in this room, which corresponded to the bed in the other on which his son lay. It was a slight paralytic seizure, the doctor said; a fit out of which he would recover probably soon. The situation altogether was so pitiful that even this stranger was moved. He took me aside, and asked where they were living, and what were the circumstances; and when I explained that they had arrived only this morning, offered to have rooms prepared in his own house, and to take them there until Mr. Campbell should have recovered. I was thankful to accept this proposal in place of anything better, finding myself in the strange position of head of this sad party, and responsible for everything; for Charlotte was entirely occupied with her father, and I could not bear that she should be disturbed by the miserable details which had now to be thought of. I had to leave her to attend to all these, but hurried back as soon as I was able to share her vigil. And I have seldom known anything so terrible as the long watch by that speechless old man; the creeping on of the endless daylight hours, the coming of the evening. She took my presence without remark, and referred to me as if I had been a brother without a word. This gave me a personal pleasure, of which I was half ashamed, at so dreadful a moment; but otherwise the day passed like a dream.

In the evening there was a stir of returning consciousness. He opened his eyes, and seemed to recognise his daughter by his side, and attempted to raise his arm, which was powerless. The inability to do this troubled him, and, perhaps, helped to rouse him. At first his speech was only a confused babble, principally of complaint and annoyance at being kept there. He seemed to think he was bound to his couch, and got very angry in his inarticulate commands to her to loose him. But, by and by, his mind took a milder mood, and his power of speech gradually came back.

"I'm thinking, I'm thinking," he said, "I've maybe been—light-headed. Where is the doctor? Maxwell, where are ye?" and he tried to turn his head to look round. Maxwell was the name of their doctor at home. Charlotte stood almost over him, in her anxiety to prevent him from seeing anything that could bring the scene of the morning to his mind; and by this time it was dark, and two wretched, flickering candles made the room difficult to decipher. He remembered something, however, of what had passed. A flicker of a smile passed over his face.

"But, Chatty, ye've—ye've found Colin?" he stammered.

"Yes, father."

"That's well—that's well! What's all that noise and shouting? It'll be the lads bringing him home."

I turned away, feeling that I could not bear it, almost afraid, excited and fatigued as I was, of making some hysterical outburst. But she could. She stood perfectly still, with her back to the light, shutting out from him as with wings all those local particulars which might have survived his recollection. She told him, with a voice that never faltered, how he must submit to be carried to bed. And, as a matter of fact, he submitted like a child, and was soon feebly interested by his removal, and refreshed by the soft air of the night that blew in his face, as we placed him in the litter to carry him away. Fortunately, the way was very short, and though there was some difficulty in getting through the crowd which had been gathered around the door for some hours, drawn together by rumours of the tragedy within, we managed it without disturbing him much. I saw him give a tremulous glance about him, and stooped down to hear what he was saying, but all that I could make out was a murmur about "A queer place London, a queer place." He had, it seemed, forgotten everything except a faint, confused idea of Colin, and that he was found and being brought home.

He fell asleep very soon after he had been settled in bed, in a comfortable room, where there was already a nurse in attendance. Then Charlotte came out to me and held out her hands. "You are tired to death," she said; "you ought to rest; but I must go back to *him*."

"Not to-night, not to-night. All this is enough to kill you. I have seen to everything."

"That I am sure of," she said, with a faint, tender smile; "and I'll not even say that I am thankful. But will you take me back? I will ask no more."

We went *back*, as she said, to the room where Colin was lying. Decency and calm had been restored to the chamber of death; the sound of hysterical crying was heard occasionally from above, increasing I thought (but I might be wrong) when it was known who was below. But below all was silent and still; a miserable candle burning, the only watch over the dead. I held up this poor light to show his face, as he lay there in all the vigour of early manhood, a frame that seemed made to resist all the storms of life. He lay as if he had been asleep, perfectly tranquil, as if shame or sorrow had never come near him. She stood silent a long time, not saying a word or shedding a tear. He had been her special companion in all their earlier days—a year younger than she, no more. I comprehended that the pang of this separation was not one to be evaporated in easy tears. I myself, who had so little to do with him, it seemed to me that every hour in which I had seen him, and every word I had ever heard him speak, came back to me in the tragic silence and gloom, only broken by the faint light which flickered in the air from the open window. A young man in the blossom of his days, with everything before him; a rich man's son, heir of all that money could buy or household love bestow—yet all concluded like this. In squalor and wretchedness, in the company of a woman not worthy to serve his sister as her maid, but made into his wife—in a horror of discovery so deep, that to escape his father's eye he rushed into God's presence with his own blood on his hands: out of the calm of existence, everyday and ordinary, what a leap into the mysterious abysses of life and death!

When Charlotte sank down on her knees beside the bed, I could endure it no longer, but, setting down the light, stole away into the adjoining room, the scene of the other chapter of this tragedy, and sat down there in the dark to wait for her, my head throbbing, my whole being confused and shaken. Even at such a moment other thoughts will intrude. It may be imagined that I should have felt, after so wonderful a drawing together of the bonds of intimacy, that there were no hopes I might not entertain. But this was far, far from being the case. Had I ever ventured to imagine that she could detach herself from all the hands that clung to her, and come into my life and become a portion of me? If so, I saw now the utter madness of the thought. I stood at the window looking out upon the lamps, and the glimmer of reflection upon the pavement, which was wet with repeated showers. A few people still hung about the outskirts of a house in which a man had killed himself. The curiosity which waits upon death, especially upon violent death, gaped at the door, as if something of that mystery would be disclosed when it opened. For my part, I felt as if there was no novelty in any incident, but that this, and only this, could have happened from the beginning of time.

When we left the house of death, Charlotte clung to me with a nervous trembling which was the first sign of exhaustion she had shown. Even in her, the claims of human weakness had to be acknowledged; her firm step wavered as she descended the steps, and she was glad to have my arm for support. But the peace of that scene after the tumult of the morning had produced its effect upon her. She began to talk to me of Colin. "He was *my* brother," she said. "Don't you know a large family falls into pairs? Charley's sister died too, and since then he has been more with me; but it was always Colin and Chatty, Chatty and Colin."

"He and you will comfort each other," I said. "Charley is so good a fellow."

"Ah!" she said, "he is good, and Colin was always a trouble—but he is not Colin. Mr. Temple, if our boy had died by God's hand and not his own"—She paused a little and trembled, and her voice died away in her throat. "I could almost have been glad," she added afterwards, with a sudden energy. "He and his life were never at harmony." I felt her whole frame quiver with the long sigh of a sorrow that was past tears.

"Then it was not only this marriage?"

"Oh, can you think so little of us?" she cried. "We would have made the best of it. Me, there is nothing, nothing I would not have done. Colin's wife, she would have been sacred. And so long as she loved him"—then she made a pause. "You will hear afterwards," she said; "I know our name, our honour was in question. Oh, when you hear, do not judge him, Mr. Temple. If he did wrong, he paid for it—always twice over, in misery and pain—and now he is in God's hand."

We went on in silence after this. We walked very slowly, for she was worn out, and I should have been glad had every yard been a mile; for it seemed to me that never again would Charlotte be so much mine.

CHAPTER V

CHARLEY, for whom I had telegraphed, came next day, very anxious and miserable, with a horror of the shame and exposure which struck me in the strangest way. To be sure it was not my name which was thus held up to everybody's observation, as connected with such a catastrophe; but the catastrophe itself was so pitiful, that I scarcely could understand this special aspect in which he viewed it. He shrank even from going about the necessary business, and drew back from everybody that might by possibility recognise him. The first thing he had seen coming into London was the report in the morning paper of the inquest; and the horror of this, and the certainty that it would circulate everywhere, and make all possibility of concealment impossible, was almost more than he could bear. It was from him that I heard the whole state of the case. Colin's expenditure had been for some years back the trouble and terror of the family, and it appeared that he had plunged into speculation by way of mending this. The letters that were found half read upon his table showed of themselves how the coils of fate were closing around him. It was evident from Charley's half revelations that the case was clearly desperate for the offender, and not much less so for the family, whose name had been made use of on all hands. This came upon the young man not all in a moment, but by degrees, as Colin's letters, and various business representations from one side and another, came flowing in. On the eve of the funeral he came to me with the paleness of despair in his face. "What am I to do?" he cried. "My father is not able to pay any attention—they tell me any new shock might kill him." "Is it so very bad?" I said. "Bad? we're ruined; that is all," cried Charley. He was, as I found out afterwards, a very good man of business; but he had never had occasion to take the responsibility on his shoulders, and now, suddenly left alone, suddenly brought face to face with unexampled calamity, his self-command forsook him for the moment. Little by little he opened out to me the state of affairs. The "works" were so profitable and the business so good, that eventually everything might come right; but in the meantime he was paralysed, and did not know what to do. Mr. Campbell was in a sort of tranquil, half-childish state, not suffering much, and quite unconscious of what had happened. To consult him was impossible, and Tom and Jack were but boys, who knew little as yet of the ramifications of the business, or anything beyond the department of which they had charge. "Have you said anything to your sister?" I asked; and then poor Charley broke down. "How can I speak to Chatty?" he said; "he was always *her* brother. I cannot bide to break her heart. It is bad enough as it is—Colin gone, and all this misery—and my father knowing nothing. If she finds out all he's brought upon us, what will she do?"

"Do you think she does not know?" I said. "It was not for nothing that your brother took such dreadful means of escape. You may be sure she suspects the worst, even if she does not know."

"If I could think that!" he said. It gave him a little composure. The mere idea that there was someone to whom he could speak freely was a support. Even to talk it over with me was something. We had been to the house of death to see that all was ready for next day's melancholy business, and the sight of Mrs. Colin done up in new crape, with the white streamers of a coquettish widow's cap setting off her commonplace comeliness, had been almost more than either of us could bear. For my part, everything seemed more mysterious to me in the light of this wife. Had Colin squandered the family substance in luxurious chambers, at the feet of one of those beautiful harpies who are never satisfied with luxury, it would have been more comprehensible. But the lodgings in Bloomsbury and the landlady's daughter seemed to throw an air of burlesque upon the tragedy. The accessories ought to have been bad and vicious, not respectable and commonplace. But it seems there are many ways of courting ruin; and there must have been other unknown chapters in his life before he came to this. Perhaps, indeed, the hasty marriage, the retirement into this shabby retreat, were of themselves efforts to get back into a better way. I walked along with Charley to the house of the doctor, in which his father and sister still were, meaning to leave him there; but he clutched at my arm. "You've been through it all," he said, in a broken voice. Charlotte came down to us in the dining-room of the doctor's house, the one corresponding to that in which the first chapter of our tragedy had been enacted. She was very pale, yet greeted us with a smile. Her father was always the same—quite comfortable, suspecting nothing, now and then asking if Colin had gone home. "'The best place for him, Chatty, the best place for him,' he says to me," she said, the tears springing to her eyes, "and we must let him think so, the doctor says. He says, 'You must do the London business, Charley. We must keep it up as long as we can.'"

"If there is any business to do—or if anybody will ever trust us more," Charley said.

She had been pale enough before, but she seemed to me to grow paler, almost ghastly. "Trust us!" she said, in a faint voice. "Is it so bad as that—have we broken trust?"

"Chatty, I don't know how you'll bear it. We are ruined, I think," the young man cried.

She waved her hand as if this was nothing. "What do you mean about trust?" she asked. "Is there anything that we cannot fulfil?"

"I don't know how the 'works' are to go on. I don't know how we are to live. We are pledged and bound on every side, and I am not clever, like my father. We will have to sacrifice everything."

Chatty drew a long breath. "Then let us sacrifice everything, Charley. That is what my father would do. There need be no hesitation about that; but no, not the 'works'—we must keep the 'works.' Cannot you think of anything that will keep them going for the children's sake?" she cried. "And then think of all the poor men thrown out of work in the middle of winter!"

"We must think of ourselves, Chatty," her brother said, with a certain indignation.

"I do. They would recover in time. They are your life," she said. "Save them, if it is possible. Don't give away our life into other hands."

"Then," said Charley, drawing a long breath—he propped himself up against the mantelshelf with a sort of despairing action—"then," he said, "there is but one thing else for it, Chatty. We must sell Ellermore."

She stood and gazed at him for a moment with dilating eyes; then she suddenly sat down on the nearest chair. She wanted support of a mechanical kind, as he did. No doubt a vision of her home and all its pleasantness—the place where they had all been born, the centre of their family pride and importance and all their traditions—flashed across her. For a few minutes she made no reply. Then she made an effort to command her voice. "Well," she said faintly, "well, then, we must make up our minds to it. We must sell Ellermore."

"Chatty," cried the young man, with the tears in his eyes, "how good it is to have you to talk to! Is that what you say? Keep the 'works' and sell Ellermore? It will bring a fancy price, you know. It's not just like so many acres. Some Englishman"—

"Oh, Charley, don't torture me!" she cried, in a voice of anguish; then faintly, "The 'works' are your life. And there are so many of us—still. We must think of the boys and the little ones—next after our honour and my father's name."

"That was what I thought," said Charley, "but I was afraid to say it. I thought you would cry out, Ellermore! Ellermore! and let the 'works' take care of themselves."

She looked up at him with a faint smile. "I never knew you took me for a fool before. I suppose it is because I am a woman."

"Chatty, don't say that!" cried the young man loudly. Such a suggestion begins to rouse the wrath of young men. He almost forgot the gravity of the position in his annoyance.

She went on musingly: "Ellermore means happiness, but the 'works' mean life. Life we must have, till—till it is taken away," she added, with a shiver; "but happiness! oh yes, it will come back. I am not so young or so ignorant as not to know that it will come back, and for all the young ones, soon, soon! There will be you and me will think a little longer, Charley, and me longest of all, but not for ever. But at present we are not happy. We will escape something—the pitying, and the sympathy, and the inquiries—at least we shall escape all that. I am sure my father would think so. But how we are to tell him I don't know," she cried again. "He is quite cheerful; he is like a child; but if we take him home, and it is not Ellermore, he will know."

They had both dried their tears as they contemplated this difficulty, which neither knew how to deal with. I had been naturally left outside of this discussion; but to hear them thus debating, consulting each other, arguing on the main thing to be done, was more than I could bear. I could not but remember the happy house, with all its advantages and homely wealth— the boats on the loch, the grouse on the hills, the luxury and abundance. That door had never been shut upon the stranger or the poor. And they were so entirely to the manner born, seated in their old house among their native hills, it seemed impossible to conceive of them in another place in other circumstances. This made it all the more wonderful to perceive that neither of them hesitated a moment. The thought of how to tell their father, how to keep him in his present state of cheerful unconsciousness, moved them indeed with a pang of bewilderment; but no irresolution, no clinging to what they liked best, no outcry against the cruel fate which deprived them of their home, was in the thoughts of either. There may be people to whom this choice would seem want of feeling. To me the quiet heroism was far more touching than any heroics. I knew the wrench it would be, and I respected them all the more that neither of them made anything of this, or even paused over it, as if the sacrifice were too much. I went home, leaving them together, with a pang in my heart of powerlessness to help them. I wonder whether the very rich are ever worked upon by those burning desires to help, to step forth and act as the providence of the suffering, which so often flame up in the bosoms of the comparatively poor. I had enough for my own wants, and desired riches little, but when I thought of stepping in to their aid, of becoming their surety and helper, my heart burned within me. I thought almost hungrily of an inheritance which was coming to me, which up to this moment I had been very well content to wait for. I wonder, I repeat, if such longings never come to the very rich who could indulge them with ease and without any personal struggle. Perhaps not; or one would hear something of it. As it is, the Quixotes of private life are seldom millionaires. I could do nothing; and perhaps it was for this reason that I desired with such painful yearning what was thus absolutely out of my power.

I have to admit, amid all these most serious thoughts, a curious delusion, as I suppose I must call it, which accompanied me wherever I went. It seemed to me that I constantly met the same figure which had encountered me in the grounds at Ellermore and warned me of Colin's danger. I took myself to task about it in every way, trying to find out some unsteadiness of nerve, some functional derangement, which could account for it. But I was quite well—my mind was far too much occupied and excited to leave me any time to consider the body, which went along swiftly and easily, occupied with everything rather than itself. These, I think, are the conditions of perfect health; and I was as well as ever I had been in my life. Yet constantly I was conscious of meeting about the streets this veiled and shadowy woman. She would come towards me, so that we encountered each other, face to face, or she would go softly past me, brushing me with her dress, making all my pulses beat wildly. This occurred chiefly in the neighbourhood in which the tragedy had happened; but there were other places far enough from that in which the same strange apparition was visible. Sometimes I could perceive in her that familiar custom, the wringing of the hands, which reminded me of Charlotte. Sometimes I seemed almost to penetrate the obscurity of the veil, and recognise a face not unlike Charlotte's. I got used to this imagination. I persuaded myself that it was nothing but an impression on my brain, which I could not get rid of, but which was altogether illusory. Though why my heart should leap up in me, and all my pulses throb, because of a thing which was nothing, I could not understand. The last time I thought I saw her was by the grave in which, with a silent misery beyond words, we laid poor Colin. Charley and I alone accompanied him to that last resting-place. Our friend the doctor had managed, I cannot tell how, to keep the wife and her family from attending, as they had all intended to do, in full panoply of woe. He told them, I don't know what—that it was a thing ladies of social importance never did, a point upon which Mrs. Colin was very susceptible—or some other argument of this description. Anyhow, he succeeded in keeping any such vulgarising element away from the simple ceremonial of the funeral. We followed him alone, Charley and I. Charlotte did not dare to leave her father for so long a time without explanation, and Charley shrank with a painful susceptibility from the sight of everybody he knew. Without any of that mocking garniture of flowers which has become a matter of fashion and vanity, without any indifferent retinue, we two stood by the grave, the young brother with a heart-breaking control of grief, and I with all the reverence of a pity scarcely less heart-rending. When I lifted my eyes from the "deep-delved" bed of utter silence and quiet, I thought I saw her standing by the edge of it, wringing her hands. The sound of a stifled sob from Charley called my attention away for a moment, and when I looked again she was gone. The face—the gesture was like Charlotte. It is impossible for me to describe the mingled tenderness and terror with which I perceived this—as if it might have been Charlotte herself in the spirit who had come forth in sheer longing to her brother's grave.

"Did you see that lady?" I asked Charley, as we went home.

"What lady?" he said fretfully. He was irritable with grief, and misery, and shame; for he had never been able to get over this accessory of the terrible family misfortune, and his mind, poor fellow, was distracted with thinking what to do, and how to manage the complicated business which had come into his hands. Then he begged my pardon piteously. "I don't know what I'm doing. To think yon was Colin, and that's all over with him—him that had more head than us all put together; and if he had only held his hand might have put all right. I would have set my strength to his," cried the young fellow, unable to restrain himself, "shoulder to shoulder; and we would have redeemed everything." Then, after a pause, during which he turned away his head to dash off the hot, quick gathering tears, "Did you say there was a lady? I took no notice. It would be his wife."

I did not say anything more; but I knew very well it was not Colin's wife. Who was it? or was it nothing more than a delusion, the offspring of my own overwrought and excited brain?

In a few days after I went to the railway with them to see them go away. Mr. Campbell had never mended more than he did the first night. His hand and one side were almost without power, and his mind had fallen into a state which it would be cruel to call imbecility. It was more like the mind of a child recovering from an illness, pleased with, and exacting constant attention. Now and then he would ask questions innumerable. What had become of Colin, if he was ill, if he had gone home? "The best place for him, the best place for him, Chatty," he would repeat; "and if you got him persuaded to marry, that would be fine." All this Charlotte had to bear with a placid face, with gentle agreement; and now that Charley was here, I had passed altogether from his mind. When he saw me he made me little apologies about not being in a state to receive strangers. "You see, I am recovering from a severe illness," he would say. "Tell Mr. Temple, Chatty, how ill I have been." He was in this condition when I took leave of him in the invalid carriage they had secured for the journey. They had all the habits of luxury, and never hesitated, as people accustomed to the daily sacrifices of poverty would have done, at this expense. He told me that he was glad to go home; that he would have left London some time before but for Chatty, who "wanted to see a little of the place." "I am going to join my son Colin, who has gone home before us—isn't that so, Chatty?" "Yes, father," she said. "Yes, yes; I have grown rather doited, and very, very silly,"[B] the old man said, in a tone of extraordinary pathos. "I am sometimes not sure of what I am saying; but Chatty keeps me right. Colin has gone on before; he has a grand head for business; he will soon set everything right—connected," he added, with a curious sense which seemed to have outlived his other powers, that explanation of Colin's actions was necessary—"connected with my retirement. I am past business; but we'll still hope to see you at Ellermore."

At Ellermore! Charlotte raised her eyes to mine with a look of anguish, of self-control, and steadfast patience, which was almost sublime. While he spoke thus her hands sought and clasped each other with the same movement I had noted in another. In another—in whom?

CHAPTER VI

THEN there ensued a period of total stillness in my life. It seemed to me as if all interest had gone out of it. I resumed my old occupations, such as they were, and they were not very engrossing. I had enough, which is perhaps of all conditions of life, if the most comfortable, the least interesting. If it was a disciple of Solomon who desired that state, it must have been when he was like his master, *blasé*, and had discovered that both ambition and pleasure were vanity. There was little place or necessity for me in the world. I pleased myself, as people say. When I was tired of my solitary chambers, I went and paid visits. When I was tired of England, I went abroad. Nothing could be more agreeable, or more unutterably tedious, especially to one who had even accidentally come across and touched upon a real and bustling life. Needless to say that I thought of the household at Ellermore almost without intermission. Charlotte wrote to me now and then, and it sometimes seemed to me that I was the most callous wretch on earth, sitting there watching all they were doing, tracing every step and vicissitude of their trouble in my own assured well-being. It was monstrous, yet what could I do? They would not have accepted the help of my small sufficiency. But if, as I have said, such impatient desire to help were to come now and then to those who have the power to do so, is political economy so infallible that the world would not be the better for it? There was not a word of complaint in Charlotte's letters, but they made me rage over my impotence. She told me that all the arrangements were being completed for the sale of Ellermore, but that her father's condition was still such that they did not know how to communicate to him the impending change. "He is still ignorant of all that has passed," Charlotte wrote, "and asks me the most heart-rending questions; and I hope God will forgive me all that I am obliged to say to him. We are afraid to let him see anyone lest he should discover the truth; for indeed falsehood, even with a good meaning, is always its own punishment. Dr. Maxwell, who does not mind what he says when he thinks it is for his patient's good, is going to make believe to send him away for change of air; and this is the artifice we will have to keep up all the rest of his life to account for not going back to Ellermore." She wrote another time that there was every hope of being able to dispose of it by private bargain, and that in the meantime friends had been very kind, and the "works" were going on. There was not a word in the letter by which it could have been divined that to leave Ellermore was to the writer anything beyond a matter of necessity. She said not a word about her birthplace, the home of all her associations, the spot which I knew was so dear. There had been no hesitation, and there was no repining. Provided only that the poor old man, the stricken father, deprived at once of his home and firstborn, without knowing either, might be kept in that delusion—this was all the exemption Charlotte sought.

And I do not think they asked me to go to them before they left the place. It was my own doing. I could not keep away any longer. I said to Charlotte, and perhaps also to myself, by way of excuse, that I might help to take care of Mr. Campbell during the removal. The fact was that I could not stay away from her any longer. I could have risked any intrusion, thrust myself in anyhow, for the mere sake of being near her and helping her in the most insignificant way.

From the time of their leaving London, the appearance I had seen so often had disappeared. I need not say that I thought upon it often enough to have raised up—had it been dependent upon my thoughts—appearances in any number; but this one never came again. I tried in my own mind every way to account for it. That it was a mere delusion of my excited eyes and brain I could not believe, for I had been aware of no excitement or reason for it when I first saw her in the shrubbery at Ellermore; and if imagination was enough to produce such an image, how much more reason was there now that it should have come back to me! And then I thought, which gave me a certain pleasure, of a possibility which had occurred to me, that Charlotte's anxious heart and thoughts had somehow assumed a shadowy form, a sort of veil of substance, and that it was she herself unawares who had haunted me. If our deepest thoughts could thus take form, how often, when we ourselves were elsewhere, might a visionary shadow of us be about those we love? It would be little wonder, I said to myself, if Charlotte were to see *me*, under the trees or by the loch side at Ellermore. Often and often, seated in my rooms, I had been there in the spirit following her, remembering what she would probably be doing at that moment, flitting after her from room to room. This was a solution of the mystery that was very sweet to me. I said to myself, it might very well be that only to one entirely in sympathy with the spirit thus gone out of itself in passionate yearning could it be visible in its love-pilgrimage. Therefore I felt, with a subdued humility, that it was very unlikely she would see any adumbration of my longing and lingering about her; but that I should see her was very natural. And this explained so entirely why I saw nothing now. It was not me she had been thinking of, but of Colin, both living and dead—all the dreadful tragedy of his soon-ended story. If she had ever admitted me to any such place in her thoughts, no doubt I should have seen her now.

I do not give this as a theory by which such apparitions might be accounted for, I only state it as one of the many thinkings on the subject which filled my mind, and the one which gave me most pleasure. I thought that nobody save Charlotte herself—not even a visitor out of the unseen— could have so made my heart beat; but it was all fanciful, founded upon nothing, a supposition among so many other suppositions. It was nearly Christmas when the insistence of myself with myself that I could stay away no longer came to a crisis. They were to leave Ellermore in a week or two. Mr. Campbell had been persuaded that one of the soft and sheltered spots where Scotch invalids are sent in Scotland would be better for him. Charlotte had written to me, with a half despair, of the difficulties of their removal. "My heart almost fails me," she said; and that was a great deal for her to say. After this I could hesitate no longer. She was afraid even of the revival of life that might take place when her father was brought out of his seclusion, of some injudicious old friend who could not be staved off, and who might talk to him about Colin. "My heart almost fails me." I went up to Scotland by the mail train that night, and next day, while it was still not much more than noon, found myself at Ellermore.

What a change! The heather had all died away from the hills; the sun-bright loch was steely blue; the white threads of water down every crevice in the mountains were swollen to torrents. Here and there on the higher peaks there was a sprinkling of snow. The fir trees were the only substantial things in the nearer landscape. The bushes stood about all bare and feathery, with every twig distinct against the blue. The sun was shining almost as brightly as in summer, and scattered a shimmer of reflections everywhere over the wet grass, and across the rivulets that were running in every little hollow. The house stood out among all this light, amid the bare tracery of the trees, with its Scotch-French *tourelles*, and the sweep of emerald lawn, more green than ever at its feet, with all the naked flower-beds; the blue smoke rising peacefully into the air, the door open as always. There was little stir or movement, however, in this wintry scene. The outdoor life was checked. There was no son at home to leave traces of his presence. The lodge was shut up and vacant. I concluded that the carriage had been given up, and all luxuries, and the coachman and his family were gone. But this was all the visible difference. I was received by one of the maids, with whose face I was familiar. There had never been any wealth of male attendants at Ellermore, and this did not strike me as unusual. She took me into the drawing-room, which was deserted, and bore a more formal look than of old. "Miss Charlotte is mostly with her papa," the woman said. "He is very frail, but just wonderful contented, like a bairn. She's always up the stair with the old gentleman. It's no' good for her. You'll find her white, white, sir, and no' like hersel'."

In a few minutes Charlotte came in. There was a gleam of pleasure (I hoped) on her face, but she was white, white, as the woman said; worn and pale. After the first greeting, which had brightened her, she broke down a little, and shed a few hasty tears, for which she excused herself, faltering that everything came back, but that she was glad, glad to see me! And then she added quickly, that I might not be wounded, "It has come to that, that I can scarcely ever leave my father; and to keep up the deception is terrible."

"You must not say deception."

"Oh, it is nothing else; and that always punishes itself. It is just the terror of my life that some accident will happen; that he will find out everything at once." Then she looked at me steadily, with a smile that was piteous to see, "Mr. Temple, Ellermore is sold."

"Is it so—is it so?" I said, with a sort of groan. I had still thought that perhaps at the last moment something might occur to prevent the sacrifice.

She shook her head, not answering my words, but the expression of my face. "There was nothing else to be desired," she said; and, after a pause, "We are to take him to the Bridge of Allan. He is almost pleased to go; he thinks of nothing further—oh, poor old man, poor old man! If only I had him there safe; but I am more terrified for the journey than I ever was for anything in my life."

We talked of this for some time, and of all the arrangements she had made. Charley was to come to assist in removing his father; but I think that my presence somehow seemed to her an additional safeguard, of which she was glad. She did not stay more than half an hour with me. "It will be dull, dull for you, Mr. Temple," she said, with more of the lingering cadence of her national accent than I had perceived before—or perhaps it struck me more after these months of absence. "There is nobody at home but the little ones, and they have grown far too wise for their age, because of the many things that they know must never be told to papa; but you know the place, and you will want to rest a little." She put out her hand to me again. "And I am glad, glad to see you." Nothing in my life ever made my heart swell like those simple words. That she should be "glad, glad" was payment enough for anything I could do. But in the meantime there was nothing that I could do. I wandered about the silent place till I was tired, recalling a hundred pleasant recollections. Even to me, a stranger, who a year ago had never seen Ellermore, it was hard to give it up; and as for those who had been born there, and their fathers before them, it seemed too much for the cruellest fate to ask. But nature was as indifferent to the passing away of the human inhabitants, whose little spell of a few hundred years was as nothing in her long history, as she would have been to the falling of a rock on the hillside, or the wrenching up of a tree in the woods. For that matter, of so small account are men, the rock and tree would both have been older dwellers than the Campbells; and why for that should the sun moderate his shining, or the clear skies veil themselves? Afterwards I went in and wandered about the house, which was so silent. A subdued sound indeed came from the children's rooms, and when I knocked at the door I was received with a tumult of delight; but next moment little Mary lifted her small finger and said, "Oh, Harry! oh, Katie! how can you make a noise and disturb papa!" The old man in his chamber dominated the whole house; the absolute quiet of it and desertion (when the children went out for their afternoon walk) had an indescribable effect upon my mind. It was as if the chamber, still and clean, all garnished and decked as for daily living, yet empty of all visible life, was full of beings unseen, for whom and for whose pleasure they existed. A kind of awe stole over me when I sat down in one of these rooms. I felt myself out of place there—as if all the solemn visitors in their old house must resent the presence of a stranger. Yes, I was a stranger; even Charlotte herself had called me so, though no one had been so near to her, or had so much to do with her life in the last crisis. It gave me a sort of bitter pleasure to think this, even though I might be disowned by those others, as having nothing to do with the house.

My mind was so taken up by these thoughts that it was almost inadvertence that took me, in the course of my solitary rambles about, to the Lady's Walk. I had nearly got within the line of the birch trees, however, when I was brought hurriedly back to the strange circumstances which had formed an accompaniment to their family history. It gave me a shock and start to hear once more the footsteps of the guardian of Ellermore. She had come back, then! After that first thrill of instinctive emotion this gave me a singular pleasure. I stood between the trees and heard the soft step coming and going with absolute satisfaction. It seemed to me that they were not altogether abandoned so long as she was here. My heart rose in spite of myself. I began to speculate on the possibility even yet of saving the old house. I asked myself how it could be finally disposed of without Mr. Campbell's consent and signature; and tried to believe that at the last moment some way might open, some wonderful windfall come. But when I turned back to the house, this fantastic confidence naturally failed me. I began to contemplate the other side of the question—the new people who would come in. Perhaps "some Englishman," as Charley had said with a certain scorn; some rich man, who would buy the moors and lochs at many times their actual value, and bring down, perhaps, a horde of Cockney sportsmen to banish all quiet and poetry from Ellermore. I thought with mingled pity and anger of what the Lady would do in such hands. Would she still haunt her favourite walk when all whom she loved were gone? Would she stay there in forlorn faithfulness to the soil, or would she go with her banished race? Or would she depart altogether, and cut the tie that had bound her to earth? I thought—for fancy once set out goes far without any conscious control from the mind—that it might be possible that the intruders into the home of the Campbells should be frightened by noises and apparitions, and all those vulgarer powers of the unseen of which we hear sometimes. If the Lady of Ellermore would condescend to use such instruments, no doubt she might find lower and less elevated spirits in the unseen to whom this kind of play would be congenial. I caught myself up sharply in this wandering of thought, as if I were forming ideas derogatory to a dear friend, and felt myself redden with shame. She connect her lovely being with tricks of this kind! I was angry with myself, as if I had allowed it to be suggested that Charlotte would do so. My heart grew full as I pursued these thoughts. Was it possible that some mysterious bond of a kind beyond our knowledge connected her with this beloved soil? I was overawed by the thought of what she might suffer, going upon her solitary watch, to see the house filled with an alien family; yet, perhaps, by and by, taking them into amity, watching over them as she had done over her own, in that sweetness of self-forgetfulness and tender love of humankind which is the atmosphere of the blessed. All through this spiritual being was to me a beatified shadow of Charlotte. I felt that this was what she might be capable of doing, if it were possible that those whom she loved most were no longer dependent upon her care.

You will say all this was very fantastic, and I do not deny that the sentence is just.

Next day passed in something the same way. Charlotte was very anxious. She had wished the removal to take place that afternoon, but when the moment came she was afraid. She said "To-morrow," with a shiver. "I don't know what I am afraid of," she said, "but my heart fails me—my heart fails me." I had to telegraph to Charley that it was deferred, and another long day went by. It rained, and that was an obstacle. "I cannot take him away in bad weather," she said. She came downstairs to me a dozen times a day, wringing her hands. "I have no resolution," she cried. "I cannot—I cannot make up my mind to it. I feel that something dreadful is going to happen." I could only take her trembling hand and try to comfort her. "But if it must be done," I ventured to say, "you will be happier when it is over." She gave me a wild look of panic. "I don't know what I am afraid of," she said. "I wish it might be taken out of my hands." I understood her, and I made all the arrangements.

Next day, at noon, was to be the time. I ordered a carriage from the nearest town, not without feeling the risk that the old man might perceive it was not his own, and inquire into the meaning of it. Every step of the way was beset by risks; but still, if it had to be done—"if 'twere done when 'tis done, then it were well it were done quickly." Those words had haunted me before. I settled everything. I made her come out with me to get a little air in the afternoon. "You are killing yourself," I said. "It is this that makes you so nervous and unlike yourself." She consented, though it was against her will. A woman who had been all her life in their service, who was to go with them, whom Charlotte treated, as she said, "like one of ourselves," had charge of Mr. Campbell in the meantime. And I think Charlotte got a little pleasure from her unusual excursion. She was very tremulous, as if she had almost forgotten the way to walk, and leant upon my arm in a way which was very sweet to me. No word of love had ever passed between us; and she did not love me, save as she loved Charley and Harry, and the rest. I think I had a place among them, at the end of the brothers. But yet she had an instinctive knowledge of my heart. And she knew that to lean upon me, to show that she needed me, was the way to please me most. We wandered about there for a time in a sort of forlorn happiness; then, with mutual impulse, took our way to the Lady's Walk. We stood there together, listening to the steps. "Do you hear them?" said Charlotte, her face lighting up with a smile. "Dear lady! that has always been here since ever I mind." She spoke as the children spoke in the utter abandonment of her being, as if returning for refreshment to the full simplicity of accent and idiom, the soft, native speech to which she was born. "Will she stay after us, do ye think?" Charlotte said; and then, with a little start, clinging to my arm, "Was that a sound—was that a cry?"

Not a cry, but a sigh. It seemed to wander over all the woods and thrill among the trees. You will say it was only the wind. I cannot tell. To me it was a sigh, personal, heart-rending. And you may suppose what it was to her. The tears dropped from her full eyes. She said, speaking to the air, "We are parting, you and me. Oh, go you back to heaven, and let us trouble you no more. Oh, go back to your home, my bonnie lady, and let us trouble you no more!"

"Charlotte," I said, taking her arm in mine to support her. She cast me a glance, a smile, like one who could not, even in the midst of the highest thoughts, neglect or be unkind, but drew her hand away and clasped it in the other. "We are of one stock," she said, the tears always falling, "and the same heart. We are too anxious; but God is above us all. Go back to your pleasant place, and say to my mother that I will never leave them. Go away, my bonnie lady, go away! and trust us to God."

We waited, and I think she almost expected some reply. But there was none. I took her arm within mine again, and led her away trembling. The moment, the excitement had been too much for me also. I said, "You tell her to go, that she is too anxious, that she must trust you to God—and in the same breath you pledge yourself never to leave them. Do you think if God does not want her He wants you to stand between Him and them?" I grasped her arm so closely and held it so to my side in my passion that I think I almost hurt her. She gave me a startled look, and put up her hand to dry her wet eyes.

"It is very different," she said; "I am living and can work for them. It has come to me all in a moment to think that one is just like another after all. Perhaps to die does not make a woman wise any more than life does. And it may be that nobody has had the thought to tell her. She will think that she can stop any harm that is coming, being here; but if it was not God's pleasure to stop it, how could she? You know she tried," said Charlotte, looking at me wistfully; "she tried—God bless her for that! Oh, you know how anxious she was; but neither her nor me could do it—neither her nor me!"

At this moment we were interrupted by someone flying towards us from the house, calling, "Miss Charlotte, Miss Charlotte! you are wanted," in a wild and agitated tone. It was the woman who had been left in charge of Mr. Campbell, and Charlotte started at the sight of her. She drew her hand from my arm, and flew along the path. "Oh, Margaret, why did you leave him?" she said.

"It was no blame of mine," said the woman, turning, following her mistress. I hurried on too, after them, and the explanation was to both of us. "He would come down to the library; nothing would stop him. I tried all I could; but what could I do? And there is nothing to be frighted for, Miss Charlotte. Ah! I've nae breath to tell it. He is just real like himself."

Charlotte flew along the path like a creature flying for life. She paused an instant at the door of the house to beckon me to follow her. The library, the room where her father had gone, was one of those which had been partially dismantled. The pictures had been taken down from the walls, a number of books, which she meant to take with her, collected on the tables. Mr. Campbell had displaced some of the books in order to seat himself in his favourite seat. He looked at her curiously, almost with severity, as she came in anxious and breathless. He was greatly changed. He had been robust and hale, like a tower, when I first entered Ellermore, not yet six months since.

Now he had shrunken away into half his size. The coat which he had not worn for months hung loosely upon him; his white hair was long, and he wore a beard, which changed his appearance greatly. All this change had come since the time I parted with him in London, when he told me he was going to join his son Colin; but there was another change more remarkable, which I with awe, and Charlotte with terror, recognised at a glance—the prostration of his mind was gone. He looked his daughter in the face with intelligent, almost sternly intelligent, eyes.

"Oh, father, you have wanted me!" Charlotte cried. "I went out for a mouthful of air—I went out—for a few minutes"—

"Why should you not have gone out, Chatty?" he said. "And why was Margaret left in charge of me? I have been ill, I make no doubt; but why should I be watched and spied about my own house?"

She gave me a glance of dismay, and then she faltered, "Oh, not that, father—not that!"

"But I tell you it was that. She would have hindered my coming downstairs, that woman"—he gave a little laugh, which was terrible to us in the state of our feelings—"and here are you rushing in out of breath, as if there was some cause of fear. Who is that behind ye? Is it one of your brothers—or"—

"It is Mr. Temple, father," she said, with a new alarm.

"Mr. Temple," he said, with a shade of displeasure passing over his face. Then he recovered himself, and his old-world politeness. "I am glad to see ye," he said. "So far as I can remember, the house was much disorganised when you were here before, Mr. Temple. You will think we are always out of order; but I've been ill, and everything has fallen out of gear. This is not a place," he added, turning to Charlotte, "to receive a stranger in. What is all this for?" he added, in a sharp tone, waving his hands towards the books, of which some were heaped at his feet on the floor.

Once more she made a pause of dismay. "They are some books to take with us," she said; "you remember, father, we are going away."

"Going away!" he cried irritably. "Where are my letters? Where are your brothers? What are you doing with a gentleman visitor (I beg ye a thousand pardons, Mr. Temple!) and the place in such a state? It is my opinion that there is something wrong. Where are my letters? It is not in reason that there can be no letters. After being cast aside from business for a time, to have your letters kept back from you, you will allow, Mr. Temple," he said, turning to me with an explanatory air, "is irritating. It is perhaps done with a mistaken notion that I am not equal to them; but if you think I will allow myself to be treated as a child" —

He stammered a little now and then, in his anger, then made a great effort to control himself. And then he looked up at us, once more a little severely, and brought confusion to all our hopes with one simple question. "Where is Colin?" he said.

What could be more natural? Charlotte gave me one look, and stood, white as death, motionless, her fingers twisting together. How truly she had said that falsehood was its own punishment, even such falsehood as this. She had answered him with ambiguous words when he was in the state of feebleness from which he had thus awoke, and he had been easily satisfied and diverted from too close inquiry. But now she was confounded by the sudden question. She could not confront with a subterfuge her father's serious eyes; her head drooped, her hands caught at each other with a pitiful clasp, while he sat looking at her with an authoritative, but as yet unalarmed, look. All this time the door had been left ajar, and Margaret stood waiting outside, listening to all that went on, without any thought of wrong, too much interested and anxious to feel herself out of place. But when she heard this demand the woman was struck with horror. She made a step within the door. "Oh, Ellermore!" she cried. "Oh! my auld maister, dinna break her heart and mine! To hear ye asking for Colin, and Colin in his grave this four long months, poor lad, poor lad!" She threw her apron over her head as she spoke, and burst forth into loud sobs and tears. Charlotte had put out a hand to stop the revelation, but dropped it again, and stood by speechless, her head bent, and wringing her hands, a silent image of grief and guilt, as if it had been her from whom the blow came.

The old man sat and listened with a countenance growing ashy pale, and with intent eyes, that seemed to flicker as if beyond his control. He tried to speak, but in the trembling of his lips could articulate nothing. Then he slowly raised himself up and stood, pallid and dizzy, like a man on the edge of a precipice.

"My son is dead, and I knew it not," he said slowly, pausing between the words. He stood with his trembling lips falling apart, his countenance all moving and twitching, transfixed, it seemed, by a sort of woeful amaze, wondering at himself. Then he turned upon Charlotte, with a piteous appeal. "Was I told, and have I forgotten?" he asked. The humiliation of that human overthrow overpowered his re-awakened soul.

She came to him quickly, and put her arm round him. "Father dear, you were so ill, they would not let us tell you. Oh, I have known — I have known it would be so much the worse when it came."

He put her away from him, and sat down again feebly in his chair. In that dreadful moment he wanted no one. The horror of the individual humiliation, the idea that he could have heard and forgotten, was more terrible even than the dreadful novelty which thus burst upon him. "I'm glad," he said, "I'm glad," babbling with his loose lips. I shrank away, feeling it a profanation to be here, a spectator of the last mystery of nature; but Charlotte made a faint motion that kept me from withdrawing altogether. For the first time she was afraid; her heart had failed her.

For some minutes her father continued silent in his chair. The sunset had faded away, the misty twilight was falling. Margaret, guilty and miserable, but still unable altogether to subdue her sobs, shaking her white apron from her head, and looking round with a deprecating, apologetic glance, had withdrawn to the other side of the room. All was silence after that broken interchange of words. He lay back, clasping and unclasping his hands, his lips and features all moving, whether with a wish to speak or with the mere workings of emotions unspeakable, I cannot tell. When suddenly, all at once, with the voice of a strong man, loud and full, he broke out into the cry which has sounded through all the world—the utterance of every father's anguish. "Oh, Absalom, my son, my son! Would God that I had died for thee, my son, my son!"

We both rushed towards him simultaneously. He did not remark me, fortunately; but again he put Charlotte away. "What are you afraid for?" he said, almost sternly; "that I will forget again? That is not possible. Ye think sorrow kills; but no, it stings ye back to life. It stings ye back to life," he repeated, raising himself in his chair. Then he looked round him solemnly. "Margaret, my woman, come here, and give me your hand. We're partners in trouble, you and me, and never shall we part. As long as this is my house there is a place in it for you. Afterwards, when it goes to—ah! when it goes to Charley," he cried, with a sudden burst of unforeseen sobs.

Charlotte looked at me again. Her face was white with despair. How was this last news to be broken to him?

"Father," she said, standing behind him, "you are sorely tried. Will you not come back to your room and rest till to-morrow, and then you will hear all? Then we will tell you—about all that has happened"—

Her voice shook like a leaf in the wind, but she managed to show no other sign of her terror and despair. There was a long pause after this, and we stood waiting, not knowing how the moment would terminate. I believe it was the sight of me that decided it after all. A quick movement of irritation passed over his face.

"I think you are right, Chatty," he said; "I think you are right. I am not fit, in my shattered state, and with the information I have just received, to pay the attention I would like to pay"—He paused, and looked at me fixedly. "It is a great trouble to me that we have never been able to show you proper attention, Mr. Temple. You see, my son was detained; and now he is dead, and I've never known it till this moment. You will excuse a reception which is not the kind of reception I would like to give you." He waved his hand. "You were my Colin's friend. You will know how to make allowances. Yes, my dear, I am best in my own chamber. I will just go, with Mr. Temple's permission—go—to my bed."

A faint groan burst from him as he said these words; a kind of dreary smile flickered on his lips. "To my bed," he repeated; "that is all we can do, we old folk, when we are stricken by God's hand. Lie down, and turn our faces to the wall—our faces to the wall." He rose up, and took his daughter's arm, and made a few steps towards the door, which I was holding open for him. Then he turned and looked round with the air of one who has a favour to bestow. "You may come too, Margaret," he said. "You can come and help me to my bed."

This strange interruption of all plans, which it was evident filled Charlotte with despair, gave me much to think of, as I stayed behind in the slowly darkening room. It was evident that now nothing could be concealed from him; and who was there so bold as to tell the bereaved father, in his first grief for his firstborn, what horrors had accompanied Colin's death, and what a penalty the family had to pay? I cast over in my mind every expedient, but nothing seemed practicable, no way of disclosing the situation without such a shock as might kill. The half-dismantled room looked more and more dreary as the light faded away. The door stood open as when that little procession quitted it. My senses were all on the alert. It seemed to me that the premonition of some fresh calamity was in the air; and when Charlotte came down about half an hour later, like a ghost through the dim-coming shadows, I almost expected to hear that it had already occurred. But even in these depths of distress, it was a happiness to me to feel that she came to me for relief. She dropped into a chair close by the window where I was standing. I could just see the soft, pale lines of her face—the look of restrained anxiety in her eyes. She told me that he had gone to bed without asking any further questions, and that Margaret, who had been Colin's nurse, seemed almost more agreeable to him than herself. He had turned his face to the wall, as he had said, and nothing but a long-drawn, occasional sigh told that he was awake. "I think he is not worse—in body," she said. "He has borne it far better than we could have thought possible. But how am I to tell him the way it happened, and how am I to tell him about Ellermore?" She wept with a prostration and self-abandonment which alarmed me; but she stopped my remonstrances and entreaties with a motion of her hand. "Oh, let me cry! It is the only ease I have," she said.

When she had gone away from me, restless, anxious, afraid to be out of hearing, I went out, myself, as restless, as incapable of banishing all these anxieties from my mind as she. The night was almost dark, soft and mild. It was one of those nights when the moon, without being visible, softens and ameliorates the gloom, and makes of night a sort of twilight.

While I went pacing softly about, to occupy myself, a soft, small rain began to fall; but this did not affect me in any way. It was rather soothing than disagreeable. I went down to the side of the loch, where the pale light on the water was touched by innumerable droppings of the rain; then up again, round and round the house, not caring where I went. At this hour I had always avoided the Lady's Walk, I can scarcely tell why. To-night, in my strange familiarity with everything, and carelessness of all but one subject, I suddenly turned into it with a caprice I could not account for, perhaps with an understood wish for company, for somebody who might understand my thoughts. The mystic footsteps gave me a sort of pleasure. Whether it was habit, or some new sense of human fellowship which Charlotte's impassioned words had caused, I can scarcely tell; but the excitement with which I had always hitherto regarded the mysterious watcher here was altogether gone out of my mind. I felt a profound and tender pity for her rising in me instead.

Was it possible that a spirit could be "over-anxious," as Charlotte said, endeavouring vainly, and yet not undutifully, to take God's supreme guardianship out of His hands? The thought was new to me. To think that a good and blessed creature could so err, could mistake so humanly and persevere so patiently, though never able to remedy the evils, seemed somehow more possible than that a guardian from heaven could watch and watch for generations with so little result. This gave me a great compassion for the lonely watcher thus rebelling in a heavenly way of love against the law of nature that separated her from visible life. My old idea that it might be Charlotte herself in an unconscious shadow-shape, whose protecting, motherly love made these efforts unawares, glided gratefully into the feeling that it was an earlier Charlotte, her very kin and prototype, who could not even now let God manage her race without her aid.

While I was thus thinking, I was startled once more by the same sigh which I had heard with Charlotte. Yes, yes, it might be the wind. I had no time to bandy explanations with myself. It was a soft, long sigh, such as draws the very breath out of an over-laden bosom. I turned half round, it was so near to me, and there, by my side, so close that I could have touched her, stood the Lady whom I had imagined so often—the same figure which I had met in the London streets and in the woods of Ellermore. I suppose I stepped back, with a little thrill of the old sensations, for she seemed to put out a hand in the pale gloom, and began to speak softly, quickly, as if there was scarcely time enough for what she had to say.

"I am going away like the rest," she said. "None of them have ever bid me go before; but it was true—it was true. I have never done any good—just frightened them, or pleased them. It is in better hands—it is in better hands."

With this there came the familiar movement, the wringing of the hands, which was like Charlotte, and she seemed to weep; but before I could say anything (and what could I have said?) she said again mournfully, "I must not speak to them; but you wish them well, and you may help if you will—if you will—now, again, again!"

"How can I help?" I cried. "Tell me, Lady, whoever you are; I will do it. I will do it—but how can I do it? I have no power. Tell me"—

I put out my hand to touch her dress, but it melted out of my hold. "You may help if you will—if you will," she seemed to say, with a breathless faintness, as if of haste; and already her voice was farther off, breathing away.

"What can I do?" I cried. So much had I forgot the old terror that I put myself in her path, stopping the way. "Tell me how, how! Tell me, for God's sake, and because of Charlotte."

The shadowy figure seemed to retreat before me. It seemed to fade, then reappeared, then dissolved altogether into the white dimness, while the voice floated away, still saying, as in a sigh, "If you will, if you will." I could hear no more. I went after this sighing voice to the end of the walk. It seemed to me that I was pursuing her, determined to understand, and that she softly fled; the footsteps hurrying, becoming almost inaudible as they flew before me. I went on hotly, not knowing what I did, determined only to know what it was; to get an explanation, by what means I did not care. Suddenly, before I knew, I found my steps stumbling down the slope at the farther end, and the pale water alive with all the dimplings of the rain appearing at my very feet. The steps sank upon the loch side, and ceased with a thrill like the acutest sound in a silence more absolute than any I have heard in nature. I stood gasping, with my foot touching the edge of the water; it was all I could do to arrest myself there.

I hurried back to the house in a state of agitation which I cannot describe. It was partly nervous dread. I do not disguise this; but partly it was a bewildered anxiety and eagerness to know what it was that I might be able to do. That I had the most absolute faith in it I need hardly say. One does not have, or think one has, such an interview as this without believing what is told in it. There was no doubt in my mind, save an anxious, excited wonder—how was it, how could it be? I searched all my horizon for possibilities. Before I reached the house, I had forgotten all the other incidents in my eagerness about this. My pursuit of her seemed nothing but natural, and the sudden silence that had seemed to tingle and thrill about me went clean out of my mind. "You may help if you will! if you will!" I said it over and over to myself a thousand times with a feverish hurry and eagerness. Indeed, I did nothing but repeat it. I could not eat, I could not rest. When Charlotte came down late to tell me her father was asleep, that the doctor who had been sent for had pronounced his recovery real, I was walking up and down the half-lighted drawing-room repeating these wonderful words over and over to myself.

"He says it is wonderful, but it may be complete recovery," Charlotte said; "only to tell him nothing we can help, to keep all the circumstances from him; especially, if it is possible, about Ellermore. But how is it possible? how can I do it? 'Help if you will?' Mr. Temple, what are you saying?"

"It is nothing," I said; "some old rhyme that has got possession of me."

She looked very anxiously into my face. "Something else has happened? You have seen or heard"—Her mind was so alive to every tone and glance that it was scarcely possible to conceal a thought from her.

"I have been in the Walk," I said, "and, being excited and restless, it was more than my nerves could bear."

She looked at me again wistfully. "You would not deceive me, Mr. Temple," she said; then returned to her original subject. The doctor was anxious, above all things, that Mr. Campbell should leave Ellermore to-morrow; that he should go early, and, above all, that he should not suspect the reason why. She had the same dread of the removal as ever, but there was no alternative; and not even a day's delay was to be thought of, for every day, every hour, made the chances of discovery more.

"But you cannot keep up the delusion for ever," I said, "and what when it is found out?"

Again she wrung her hands. "It is against my judgment; but what can I do?" She paused a moment, and then said, with a melancholy dignity, "It can but kill him, soon or syne. I would not myself have my life saved by a lie; but I am weak where my father is concerned, and God understands all. Oh, I am beginning to feel that so, Mr. Temple. We search and search, and think what is best, and we make a hundred mistakes; but God sees the why and the wherefore. Whoever misunderstands, He never misunderstands."

She went away from me in the calm of this thought—the secret of all calm. It seemed to me that I, in my blind anxiety, guessing at the enigma that had been given to me, and my poor Lady vagrant from the skies, still trying to be the providence of this house, were left alike behind.

I could not rest all night. It was all I could do to remain in my room after the diminished household had gone to rest. It was a weird night, lighted up by that mystic light of the waning moon, in which there seems to be always something that is baleful and prophesies evil. One can fancy evil creatures about, ill dews falling. I sat at my window, as often as I could persuade myself to keep still at all, with the damp air saturating me, and the cold light enveloping everything below in a whiteness and blackness of exaggerated contrast. I can say nothing less than that I expected to see the anxious, wistful figure which I had seen so often, looking up at me, appealing to me again. But nothing broke the blank of the white light; nothing but the shadow of the bare trees, outlined in every twig above the darkness of the shrubberies below, interrupted the shining of the moon. When I threw myself upon my bed, it was only to think more acutely, more restlessly than before. What was it that I could do? How could I help them? What power of mine could save? The dull morning was a relief to me which I cannot describe, and to hear the first stirrings of the household. Now at least there would be something which I could do—something not lying vague and shadowy among the possibilities, but certain and feasible, which is of all things the greatest relief to anxious thought. Charlotte came down to breakfast with me, which she had not done before. She told me that her father had passed a good night, that he had shed tears on awaking, and begun to talk tenderly and calmly of Colin; and that everything seemed to promise that the softening and mournful pre-occupation of grief, distracting his mind from other matters, would be an advantage to him. It was pleasant to be left with Margaret, who had adored her nursling, and who had been fully warned of the necessity of keeping silence as to the circumstances of his death. The post-bag came in while we were talking. It lay on the table for a few minutes untouched, for neither of us were anxious for our correspondence. We were alone at table, and Charlotte had rested, though I had not, and was almost cheerful now that the moment had arrived for the final severance. The necessity of doing inspirited her, as it did me. And perhaps, though I scarcely dared to think so, this tranquil table at which we sat alone, which might have been our table, in our home, in a new life full of peace and sober happiness, soothed her. The suggestion it conveyed made the blood dance in my veins. For the moment, it seemed as if the hope I dared not even entertain, for one calm hour of blessedness and repose, had come true.

At last she gave me the key, and asked me to open the bag. "I have been loth to disturb this peaceful moment," she said, with a smile which was full of sweetness and confidence, "and nothing outside seems of much consequence just now; but the boys may have something to tell, and there will be your letters. Will you open it, Mr. Temple?" I, too, was loth—more loth than she—to disturb the calm; and the outside world was nothing to me, while I sat here with her, and could fancy her my own. But I did what she told me.

Letters are like fate; they must be encountered, with all that is good and evil in them. I gave her hers, and laid out some, probably as important to them, though they seemed to me so trifling and unnecessary, that were for the maids. Then I turned to my own share. I had two letters, one with a broad black border, which had been forwarded from one place to another in search of me, and was nearly ten days old—for, like most people, I examined the outside first; the other a large, substantial blue letter, which meant business. I can remember now the indifference with which I opened them, the mourning envelope first. There were so many postmarks on it, that that of its origin, which would have enlightened me at once, never struck me at all.

Heaven above! what was this that met my eyes? An announcement, full of periphrasis, of formal regrets, of the death of my old Cousin Jocelyn ten days before. I gave a sort of fierce cry—I can hear it now—and tore open the second, the official letter. Of course I knew what it was, of course I was aware that nothing could interfere, and yet the opportuneness of the announcement was such that human nature, accustomed to be balked, would not allow me to believe in the possibility. Then I sprang from my seat. "I must go," I cried; "there is not a moment to lose. Stop all proceedings—do nothing about the going, for God's sake, till I come back."

"Mr. Temple, what has happened? Charley"—cried Charlotte, blanched with terror. She thought some other catastrophe had occurred, some still more fatal news, that I could not tell her. But I was too much absorbed in my own excitement to think of this.

"Do nothing," I said; "I will meet Charley on the way, and tell him. All will be right, all will be right; only wait till I come back." I rushed to the door in my haste, then came back again, not knowing what I did, and had caught her in my arms before I knew—not in my arms, but with my hands on her shoulders, holding her for one mad moment. I could hardly see her for the water in my eyes. "Wait," I said, "wait till I come back! Now I can do what she said! Now my time is come; do nothing till I come back." I let my hands drop down to hers, and caught them and kissed them in a wild tremor, beyond explanation. Then I rushed away. I have a recollection of meeting the children and pushing aside their little outstretched hands and morning salutations. It was a mile or more to the little quay where the morning boat carried communications back to the world. I seemed to be there as on wings, and scarcely came to myself till I descended into the noise, the haze, the roar of the damp streets, the crowds and traffic of Glasgow. Next moment (for time flew, and I with it, so that I took no note of its progress) I was in the clamour of the "works," making my way through the grime and mud of a great courtyard, with machinery lying round me on every side, amid the big skeleton houses with their open windows, into the office, where Charley, in close converse with a stranger, jumped up with terror at the sight of me. "What has happened?" he cried, "my father?" I had scarcely breath enough to say what I had to say. "Your father," I cried, "has come to himself. You can make no sale without him—every arrangement must be stopped at once." All that I was capable of knowing was, with a certainty, beyond all proof, that the man with whom Charley was talking, a sportsman in every line of his countenance and clothes, was the intending purchaser of Ellermore.

I remember little of the conversation that followed. It was stormy and excited; for neither would Charley be convinced, nor would the other consent to be off his bargain. But I made my point clear. Mr. Campbell having recovered his faculties, it was clear that no treaty could be concluded without his consent. (It would not have been legal in any case, but I suppose they had in some way got over this.) I remember Charley turning upon me with a passionate remonstrance, when, almost by violence and pertinacity, I had driven his Cockney sportsman away. "I cannot conceive what is your object, Temple," he said. "Are you mad? My father must give his consent; there is no possibility of a question about it. Ellermore must be sold—and as well to him as to another," he said, with a sigh. I took out my blue letter, which I had huddled into my pocket, and laid it before him. "It is to me that Ellermore must be sold," I said.

My inheritance had come. There was nothing wonderful about it—it was my right; but never did inheritance come at a more suitable moment. Charley went back with me that afternoon, after a hurried conference with his young brothers, who came round me, shaking my arms nearly off, and calling to each other in their soft young basses, like rolls of mild thunder, that, whatever happened, I was a good fellow, a true friend. If they had not been so bashful they would have embraced me, less, I verily believe, from the sense of escape from a great misery which they had scarcely realised, than from generous pleasure in what they thought a sort of noble generosity.

That was their view of it. Charley perhaps was more enlightened. He was very silent during the journey, but at one point of it burst out suddenly upon me. "You are doing this for Chatty, Temple. If you take her away, it will be as bad as losing Ellermore." I shook my head. Then, if never before, I felt the hopelessness of the position. "There is but one thing you can do for me: say not a word of that to her," I said.

And I believe he kept counsel. It was of her own accord that Charlotte came up to me after the hurried interview in which Charley laid my proposal before her. She was very grave, though the sweetness of her look drew the heart out of my breast. She held out her hands to me, but her eyes took all warm significance out of this gesture. "Mr. Temple," she said, "you may think me bold to say it, but we are friends that can say anything to one another. If in your great generosity there may yet be a thought—a thought that a woman might recompense what was done for her and hers"—Her beautiful countenance, beautiful in its love and tenderness and noble dignity, but so pale, was suddenly suffused with colour. She took her hands out of mine, and folded them together—"That is out of my power—that is out of my power!" she said.

"I like it better so," I cried. God help me! it was a lie, and so she knew. "I want no recompense. I will be recompensed enough to know you are here."

And so it has remained ever since, and may, perhaps, for ever—I cannot tell. We are dear friends. When anything happens in the family I am sent for, and all is told to me. And so do I with her. We know all each other's secrets—those secrets which are not of fortune or incident, but of the soul. Is there anything better in marriage than this? And yet there is a longing which is human for something more.

That evening I went back to the Lady's Walk, with a sort of painful desire to tell her, the other, that I had done her bidding, that she had been a true guardian of her race to the last. I paced up and down through the dim hour when the sun ought to have been setting, and later, long into the twilight. The rain fell softly, pattering upon the dark glistening leaves of the evergreens, falling straight through the bare branches. But no soft step of a living soul was on the well-worn track. I called to her, but there was no answer, not even the answer of a sigh. Had she gone back heart-sick to her home in heaven, acknowledging at last that it was not hers to guard her race? It makes my heart ache for her to think so, but yet it must have been a sweet grief and easily healed in those blessed regions, to know that those she loved were most safe in God's only care when hers failed—as everything else must fail.

THE SHIP'S DOCTOR

THE Gushat-house stood, as its name denotes, at the angle where two roads met. These were pleasant country roads both—one, shadowed by trees, here and there, threading through rich and broad fields, led up into the wealthy inland country, the rich heart of Fife; the other, with scattered cottages instead of the trees, growing after a while closer and closer together, was the straight road to the "town," and was open to the sea view and the sea breezes. The town was the little town of Anstruther on the Fife coast; the sea was the Firth of Forth, half ocean, half river; the time was fifty years ago. In this locality, and at that distant period, happened the very brief and simple story I have now to tell.

In the Gushat-house lived Mrs. Sinclair and Nora, her daughter. The house was, in its humble way, a kind of jointure-house, though it belonged to no potent family or county magnate. It had been for generations—since it was built, indeed—the refuge of one widow or other, who had sufficient interest in the place to remain near it, or some connection with the soil. The present occupant had been the wife of the minister, and was the daughter of one of the smaller proprietors in the neighbourhood. She was a woman whom the county did not disdain to visit and honour; but yet she was not rich nor a great lady in her own person. In those days life was simpler, more aristocratic perhaps, but less luxurious, and far more homely. Nowadays the coast towns in Fife are unendurable. In summer they are nothing but great receptacles of herrings, not in their silvery state as they come in in glistening shoals in the boats from sea, but in the hideous course of economical preservation and traffic. Salt and smells, and busy women armed with knives, operating upon the once harmless "drave," line all the stony little streets, and send up to heaven an unsavoury testimony. You breathe herrings, if you are so unwary as to trust yourself in the season on that too prolific coast. But it was not so fifty years ago. Then the herrings came in to be eaten, not to be salted down in barrels, and they had not got the upper hand of everything. There was no lucrative trade going on, no salt and pungent harvest-time of the sea; but the homely wynds were passable, even in summer, though cleanliness was far from perfect. In place of the herrings there was the whale fishery, which sent out its ships periodically, and brought back with corresponding regularity the sailor fishermen to their families when the expedition of the year was over. It was a trade more picturesque, more dangerous, and less disagreeable, at least to the bystander. Nobody could refuse to be interested in the solemn ships going forth to their struggle with the ice, and the storms, and the monsters of the sea; nor in their exciting return, when the well-known rig would heave slowly in sight on the broad Firth, under eager telescopes, which reported the signs she carried, the jubilant garland on the mast, sign of a successful fishing, or the melancholy flag half-mast high, which thrilled the whole town with alarm, no one knowing whose son or husband, or what family's father it might be. An interest almost more exciting, and certainly more frequent, would thrill through the little salt-water place when a gale came on suddenly at some time when "our boats" were at sea. So that the "town" was not without its points of human interest, before the herring barrels, and hideous trade consequent thereupon, had appeared in the stony little streets.

And to Nora Sinclair it was a very interesting place. She was fond of the fisher-folk, whom she had known all her life, and who, for their part, were fond of her. She and her mother were local princesses, as it were, in the parish; for the reigning minister was unmarried and unsympathetic. In those days, before the advent of King Herring, even the position of the minister was different. There was no dissent in the place, except the little Episcopal church, "English chapel," as it was called, to which some of the adjacent gentry came, and which everybody regarded with half indulgent, half contemptuous tolerance. It was tacitly admitted as a kind of necessity that the fine people should frequent this little conventicle. The common people granted them the indulgence with a half smile at their weakness of caste and training, but occupied the parish church themselves in close masses, filling the pews with characteristic rugged faces, and the air with a faint breath of fish and tar and salt water—the inalienable odour of a seafaring population. Nora Sinclair was in most things a young woman of refined tastes; but she had never had her eyes or her senses opened to these little imperfections. She took all the interest of a daughter of the place in its vicissitudes, and knew the boats and their crews, and was as anxious when it blew a gale as if she herself had known what it was to venture her heart on the dangerous chances of the sea. Her mother and she lived a not uncheerful life in the Gushat-house, metaphorically placed, as it was, with one eye on the country and one on the sea. The "families" about were many of them "connections" of Mrs. Sinclair, who was, as has been said, of a very good stock—old Auchintorlie's daughter; and those who were not connections were old friends. The mother and daughter were not left alone when they had to change to the wistful widow's refuge from the manse. Kind friends and cheerful company surrounded them. In the depth of winter, when the Firth was often black with storms, and the weather too gloomy for enjoyment, the two ladies would go "across" in the ferry-boat from Kinghorn to Edinburgh, not without some trembling for the dangers of the passage, and settle themselves there for a few months, during which time Nora would have her gaieties, and be taken to a few balls, and take her share in the pleasures of her youth. Altogether it was a very endurable life.

It was in Edinburgh she first met with Willy Erskine, though he was a neighbour at home. He was one of the Erskines of Drumthwacket, of as good a family as any in Fife. One of Mrs. Sinclair's perplexities was to make out in what way the Erskines and the Auchintorlie family were connected, but she never succeeded in clearing it up. That there was some connection she was sure, and Willy was very welcome when he paid those frequent visits in Heriot Row, where they were living, and sat so long that Nora grew tired of him, though he was a handsome young fellow. "Poor callant! so far away from home, what would he do but come and see me, that am his mother's near connection?" Mrs. Sinclair would say. And if she could have been angry with her Nora, it would have been for this cause.

"Not so very near, mamma," Nora would answer. "And if all our connections were to come as often" —

"They all show a very proper feeling, my dear," was her mother's reply; and nothing could be more true. Cousins to the fifth degree always turned up to take care of Nora at her balls — to dance with her when there — to cheer her mother's solitude when she was gone, according to their several ages and sexes. The Sinclairs were a very "well-connected" family, and it was a circumstance which added much to the comfort of their life.

As for Willy Erskine, he was a very nice young fellow, everybody allowed. He was not rich, to be sure. The Drumthwacket household was known not to be a rich one, and he was the third son. But he was doing what it was the proper thing for a third son to do. It had not been his vocation to go to India, like his second and fourth brothers, though, no doubt, that would have been the best way; and New Zealand and Australia had not been discovered, so to speak, in those days. His eldest brother was at the Bar, and Johnny, the fifth, was to be the clergyman of the family; so that Willy's lot was clear before him, even had he not been impelled towards it by a naturally scientific turn of mind. He was pursuing his medical studies at Edinburgh University during those years when Nora and her mother came in the winter to Heriot Row. In summer it was quite a practicable thing to walk from Drumthwacket, which was only sixteen miles off, down to Anstruther on one pretence or other — an expedition which made it quite natural as well as necessary to "look in" at the Gushat-house, somewhere near the time of the early dinner. The fare on Mrs. Erskine's table was homely, but it never occurred to her to grumble at the frequent visitor, or put on company punctilios, or even a fresh tablecloth, for Willy. The latter was a point upon which the population of the Gushat-house were always very easy in their minds; for no lady in Fife had a better stock of "napery," and none were more delicately, femininely alive to the beauties of clean linen. Besides which, everybody in those days washed at home, and clean tablecloths cost nothing—a matter of primitive luxury unknown in our days. Young Erskine would look in, and nobody was otherwise than pleased to see him; other people, too, "looked in" on other days. Sometimes there would be two or three strangers, equally unexpected and welcome at the widow's table. There was glorious fish, fresh from the sea—cod, with great milk-white flakes, and the delicious haddocks of the Firth, which cost next to nothing, to take the edge off the wholesome appetites of these young people; and savoury old Scotch dishes, such as exist no more—Scotch collops, brown and fragrant; chickens, which were not called chickens, but "hens"; dainty curries, in which the homely, rural gentry, with sons and brothers by the score in India, were as great critics as the old Indians themselves. To the board thus spread the country neighbours were always kindly welcome; and Mrs. Sinclair took no special notice of the frequency with which young Erskine made his appearance. If Nora was more observant, she was also more tolerant than she had been in Edinburgh. She did not even seem to dislike it much when chance brought her in contact with the young student among the rocks, as sometimes happened. Though that age was not so advanced as our own, it was still possible, even at so rudimentary an epoch, to make good use of the sea-coast, and the marine creatures which the young man was studying, to further such encounters. He called them by their Latin names when he walked with Nora up to the Gushat-house, and Mrs. Sinclair respected his habits of research. "It's little good he'll get out of the tangle on the rocks," she would say, "but it shows a diligent mind." At which praise Willy would blush and Nora smile.

But there was no haste, no rush upon the inevitable, no rash effort to put it to the touch, to win or lose it all. He would have lost his love altogether had he been precipitate. Nora was the only child of her mother, who was a widow. She had tender love to guard her, and full freedom to do as she pleased. She was the favourite of all the fisher-folk, the beauty of the town, admired, imitated, caressed, and followed wherever she went. The Gushat-house was the cheeriest little house in all the countryside, and Mrs. Sinclair was the most indulgent mother: naturally, therefore, Nora had no wish, not the most distant inclination, to sacrifice all this to become any man's wife. Love lays hold upon some people with a violent hand, but with others has to go softly, and eschew all turbulence. Nora began to like young Erskine's society. She began to feel a certain lightness diffuse itself over her heart when she saw him coming down the long country road, crossing the shadow of the trees. When winter came, and these same trees were bare, and the journey to Heriot Row drew near, it was a pleasure to her to remember that Erskine was already there. Not that she went so far as to form a good resolution to be kinder to him, to permit his attendance more willingly. She was only pleased to think that he would be at hand to be snubbed or encouraged as the humour might seize her—a very improper spirit, as the youthful reader will perceive. But Nora was far from being a perfect young woman. Thus things went on in a leisurely way. There was no hurry; even Willy himself, though he was deeply in earnest, was aware that there was no hurry. If any competitor should appear, ready to carry her off suddenly, then Willy Erskine would wake up too, and fly, violent and desperate, to the assault. But no such catastrophe was threatening. Nora, everybody said, was "fancy free." Even her saucy sallies, her little caprices, proved this. Her lovers were her friends, in a quaint, rural sort of way. She did not wish to cast any of them from the latter eminence by regarding them in the former capacity. She might go on wandering through the metaphorical forest for years, some people said, and take the crooked stick at the end. Whether he was the crooked stick or not, Willy Erskine, like a wise general, kept a wary eye on her tactics, and held himself ready to take advantage of any weakening in her defences. It had begun years ago, when they were boy and girl; it might last till they were middle-aged, for anything that could be said to the contrary. He was always at Nora's disposal, to do anything she chose to ask him; and she was always friendly to Willy, ready to stand up for him when he was absent, and to give him the most solemn good advice when he permitted her the opportunity. Nora might have been his grand-mother, to judge by the prudent counsel she gave him, and would try his devotion the next moment by laying upon him the most frivolous and troublesome commissions. Thus the time went on imperceptibly, marking its progress on these two at least by no remarkable events. Nora was bridesmaid so often to her youthful friends that she began to declare loudly that she had forestalled her own luck, and would never be a bride—but without any sort of faith in her own prediction. Yet, though this state of things was a very pleasant one, it was a necessity that, one time or other, it should come to an end.

The end was brought about, as it happened, by another event of great importance to young Erskine, and in which Nora and her mother, as in duty bound, took a lively interest. Willy's professional studies came to a conclusion, and the ladies went, well pleased, to witness the curious ceremonial at which he was "capped," as it is called—the outward sign and token of his having attained the dignity of M.D. He had passed his examinations with credit, and his friends were proud. At night there was a little party of Fife folk at Heriot Row. The good people went to tea and supper, and made one substantial but light, and one still more substantial and very heavy, meal. Then the health of the young doctor was drunk with kindly enthusiasm. "Willy, take you my advice and get a wife next," said one of the genial guests, and the suggestion was received with general applause.

"A doctor without a wife is like rigging without a ship," said another adviser. "There's two professions that must aye have the ballast of a petticoat. As for a soldier, like your brother Sandy, he's better without one, if he could be brought to think it; and John will be the laird, and he can take his time. But a minister and a doctor have no choice. You'll ask us to your wedding next, if you'll be guided by me."

"What Captain Maitland says is very true," said Mrs. Sinclair; "a doctor's never well received in families till he's a married man. You're but young, and there's no hurry, except for that. When I was a young woman myself, and needing doctors, not even a family connection would have led me to call in a man that was without a wife."

"Here's a man that has no mind to be without a wife," cried Willy. Perhaps he was a little excited with drinking his own health, or someone else's. "I wish it only depended on me" —

"You can but try," said one, patting him on the shoulder. "Faint heart never won fair lady," said another. "I would not wonder if it was all settled a year ago!" said a third; and various looks, some veiled, some openly significant, were turned upon the corner where, amid a little knot of girls, Nora sat apart. It was no revelation to Nora; but the thought of being thus openly indicated set her pride up in arms. She to marry Willy Erskine for any reason whatsoever except her sovereign grace and pleasure! She to take him because he was a doctor and wanted a wife! She had to dance the first reel with him, when the room was cleared after supper, and Mrs. Sinclair went to the piano—partly because he was the hero of the occasion and she the daughter of the house, partly because they were such old friends; but she would scarcely grant the young fellow a look even when her hand was in his in the pretty, animated dance. And Willy, in his excitement, held that soft hand longer and clasped it closer than was at all needful. Nora's girlish temper blazed up; but he could not see it, the foolish boy. His own heat and ardour, long suppressed, the pleasant intoxication of all those friendly plaudits and flattering good wishes, the seduction of the moment, when all were gone but himself, and the careful mistress of the house had begun to put away the remnants of the feast and lock up her "garde-vin," were too much for him. Willy was so far left to himself as to arrest Nora in the hall when she had said good-night to the last guest. He was by way of leaving himself, when he stopped her and took her hand. "Say a kind word to me, Nora," he cried, drawing her into the dimly-lighted little room behind, which was called the library. Mrs. Sinclair was in the dining-room close by, with her confidential handmaiden, putting away the things. They could hear her voice where they stood, and there was no harm in this little chance interview. "Say a kind word to me, Nora," he pleaded; "you know how fond I am of you. I've never thought of another since I was a boy at school. I've looked forward to this for years and years."

"What have you looked forward to, Mr. Erskine?" said Nora, with the insolence of power.

"Nora—Nora, don't speak like that!" cried the young man. "I'm not worth it, but you must take me—you know you must take me; you're all the world to me. What do I care for my degree or anything else but for you? Say you'll take a poor fellow, Nora! You know you are all the world to me."

"Indeed, I know nothing of the kind," said Nora. "I am very sleepy, and I don't care much about your degree. Must take you, indeed! I never do anything that I must do. What with their toasts, and their talk, and their nonsense, they've turned your head. Good-night."

And she went away from him, while he stood and looked after her stupefied. "Nora!" he said, in a voice of such pain that Mrs. Sinclair heard, and left the "things" on the table. She came in while Nora stood still, haughty and offended, at the door. The mother saw at once what was the matter. She thought it was a lover's quarrel, and she saw there had been enough of it for the night.

"I thought you had gone with the Lindsays, Willy," she said, looking at him in her motherly way; "and you must be wearied and fit for your bed. What's Nora making her little *moue* at now? But never mind her, my man; to-morrow's a new day."

"Yes, to-morrow's a new day," cried Willy. "I'll take no thought of what I've heard to-night. To-morrow I'm coming back."

And with that he rushed away. As for Nora, she flew upstairs, and went to bed, that she might not come in for that little sermon which was on her mother's lips. When she had shut herself into her own room she had a good cry. She could not have told anyone the reason of her perversity. She was angry with herself and Willy, and the guests who had put such nonsense in his head, and all the world. *Must* take him! very likely! If she, Nora Sinclair, ever had anything to say to a man who came to her with such a plea—She paused, on the verge of a petulant vow. Perhaps, on the whole, it would be as well not to make any oaths on the subject. And, luckily, at that moment she fell asleep, which was the easiest way out of the dilemma. To-morrow would be, as Mrs. Sinclair said, a new day.

But, unfortunately, to-morrow is not always a new day. When Nora got up in the chilly spring morning, she was, on the whole, rather more irritated and petulant than she had been the evening before. As for Mrs. Sinclair, it was her fixed opinion that the young folk should be left to themselves to make up their little matters. "They know each other's ways best," she said; "older folk do more harm than good when they interfere." So when Willy came in, pale and breathless, the kind woman withdrew herself that the two might get it over undisturbed. It was not a new day for young Erskine any more than it was for Nora. It was a feverish supplement to last night. He had not perhaps gone to bed calmly after all his excitement, as a girl has to do. There was a rere-supper somewhere, to which his friends had dragged him, and where, probably, Willy's brain had been heated by strong drinks. The morning found him parched with mental impatience and suspense, as well as with a certain degree of bodily feverishness and misery. It seemed to his heated eyes as if Nora meant to jilt him after all his devotion. He swore a big oath to himself as he rushed along to Heriot Row. "If she'll not take me now, after all," said Willy, "by — —! I'll go off to sea, and I'll never be heard of more."

In this mutual mood the two met. It was not an amiable interview on either side. The young lover took up precisely the line of argument which was most prejudicial to him. He pleaded his faithful services—his devotion which had lasted for years. He established a claim upon Nora, which she was not the girl to put up with. And she, on her side, scornfully denied any claim he had upon her. "If that is what you call love," said the indignant maiden, "to follow a girl about, whether she likes or not, and then to tell her she *must* take you, to pay you for it!" This, alas, was not the way of settling their affairs!

"Nora," cried the young man, desperate, "this is the moment that's to settle my life. It's little matter for you, but for me it's life or death. I'm not asking you to take me now—say a year, say even two years, I'll be content; but I have to know. Nora, bide a moment. If you turn me away without any hope, by — —! there's the *Pretty Peggy* sails from Anster on Saturday; I'll go to Greenland in her, and never see you more."

"And why should I want to see you more?" said Nora. "What do I care for your *Pretty Peggy*? It will do you a great deal of good, Mr. Erskine. It will teach you that you can't have everything your own way."

"Is this your last word, Nora?" cried the poor fellow, with glistening eyes. If she had looked him in the face, Nora's heart would have given way. But she felt her weakness, and would not look him in the face. She stood by the table, turning over and over in her hand an Indian toy of carved ivory, with her eyes fixed upon it, as if it was the intricacies of the pattern that involved life and death; and then she said slowly, while the blood seemed to ebb away from her heart, "I have nothing more to say."

In another moment the door shut violently, and Willy Erskine was gone. The sound went through the house like a thunderclap, and threw down, with its violent concussion, the castle of cards in which Nora had been entrenching herself. She sank down upon a chair, stupefied, and listened to the step that went echoing along the street. Was he gone? Was he really gone, and for ever? Gone to Greenland in the *Pretty Peggy*, into the ice where men and ships perished, into the whaling boats where they sank and were lost for ever? Should she never see him more?

"You've made the bed, and you must lie on it," said Mrs. Sinclair, when she heard all, with an indignation that was soon lost in sympathy. But Nora would not give way either to the sympathy or the indignation. She declared steadily that she would do the same over again if it was in her power. "What right had he to come making claims, and speaking of his rights to me?" she said. "If a lad follows a girl, does that give him a right to her—whether or no?" This was said with burning eyes, into which tears refused to come. But yet Nora shed tears enough over it. She took immense pains privately to find out when the *Pretty Peggy* sailed, and to know if she had shipped a doctor before she left Anster pier. Not for her life would she have asked the doctor's name, but she satisfied herself so far. And when the fact could no longer be doubted, her heart grew so sick that she could not go home. The Sinclairs had friends "in England"—a vague sort of expression used by the untravelled Scotch then, as untravelled islanders nowadays talk of "the Continent." Nora persuaded her mother that it would be pleasant to "go south," and pay the long-promised visit. She was glad to go away, glad to be anywhere out of the range of those people and places with which Willy Erskine's name was so closely connected. But the other day it seemed he had been so jubilant, so full of good prospects and high hopes. Now he was out upon the Northern seas, surgeon in a whaling ship, like any poor student or broken man. And he Drumthwacket's son! and whose fault was it all? Nora was ashamed to confront even the familiar rocks that knew him so well—that knew how she had met him (by accident), and strayed with him along the sea-verge, with the salt spray now and then dashed into their fresh faces, and the surge rising to their feet. She dragged her home-loving mother about from one "connection" to another all the summer through, enjoying the visits but little, poor child. As for Mrs. Sinclair, a British matron of the present day would not be more disconsolate, nor feel herself more alien in the heart of French society, than was this Scottish gentlewoman among her southern connections. Their ways, their accent, their mode of living, were all discordant to her. "If I were to live all my life among those English," she said, "I think I would rather die." Her soul longed for the tents of Jacob and the dwellings of Jerusalem. "But if I were not to humour my own bairn," added Mrs. Sinclair, with pathos, "who should humour her?" Nora was her only child; somehow or other she had make a mistake in her young life. Clouds had come up over the sun at the moment when that sun should have been brightest. Her mother could have given her the best of good advice, but she chose to give her something better instead — she "humoured" Nora. She was her tender partisan, right or wrong. She took up her cause and supported her silently against her own reproaches and all the world. And that is the best way of healing the wounded, if their friends but knew.

It was the end of summer before they returned to the Gushat-house. And then, whether it was that they were unexpected, or whether from her misdeeds towards Willy Erskine, as Nora thought, few people came to see them at first, and nobody so much as mentioned the Drumthwacket family. The name of Erskine was never, as Nora thought, named before her; and she felt herself more guilty still as she seemed thus to read her own condemnation in the eyes of others. But now the turn of the season had arrived; when she cast wistful looks from the corner of the garden up the long country road, going "north," as those geographical, seafaring populations described it, a leaf would now and then flicker down through the sunny air, a sign that autumn had come. A few weeks more, and the *Pretty Peggy* might flutter up the Firth with all her sails set, like a fine lady coming into a ballroom, as the sailors delighted to say; and if Nora, penitent, with softness in her eyes, were by, could anyone doubt that the eager face of the ship's doctor would expand too, and that the evil days would come to an end? No one could have doubted it but Nora. It was as certain that it would all be made up as that the *Pretty Peggy* would come safe out of the icy seas. To be sure, ships were lost there sometimes, sometimes detained among the ice. But look what a season it has been! Even the men's wives were easy in their minds, and sung by their wheels, or mended the nets at their cottage doors, and looked over the smooth Firth with contented hearts. A week or two more, and the seamen, with their wages, and their curiosities, and their rejoicing, would have come home.

There was not a man's wife in the *Pretty Peggy* who was so anxious as Nora. But then it was *her* fault. It was she who had sent him to sea—he who was no seaman, he whom a wealthier lot awaited. And perhaps he would look bitterly upon the woman whose caprice had wrought him so much harm. This was the thought that made her heart ache, and made the days so long to her. She used to walk out to the pier to watch the sunset reflections, and listen in silence to the prognostications of the fishers and seamen about. When they prophesied a gale, Nora's heart would beat wild with alarm; when they gave their word the storm was past, a hush as of a consoled child would come over her. At last there came a speck on the horizon, upon which all those ancient mariners fixed their telescopes. They exchanged opinions about her rig, and her hull, and her manner of sailing, till Nora, standing by, was half crazed with suspense. At last the news flew through the town, waking up all the wynds and cottages. It was the *Pretty Peggy* at last.

It would be vain to describe the excitement into which Nora, like many another woman, rose at the news. The other women were the sailors' wives, who had a right to be moved. She had no such right. She had never spoken even to her mother of the *Pretty Peggy*. She had been too proud at first to betray the smallest interest in the movements of her lost love, and she did not even know whether Mrs. Sinclair was aware that Willy was coming with the returning seamen out of the icy seas. She had to invent a reason for her anxiety as the ship drew near the port. "Willy Morrison is in her, mamma," said Nora. "I'd like to go down and see them come in. His mother will be so happy." Willy Morrison's mother had been Nora's nurse, and that was her excuse.

"Well, well," said Mrs. Sinclair, with an impatience unusual to her. "I wanted you at home this afternoon; but Nancy will be proud to see you have a warm heart to your foster-brother. Be home as soon as you can. I would not be surprised if some friend was to look in to tea."

Nora gave her mother a startled look, of which Mrs. Sinclair took no notice. She looked as if she had her secret too; and most probably she knew as well as her daughter did who was coming up the tranquil Firth in the returning ship. Did her mother expect him too? Could it be possible, after all the tragic hours that were past, that things should fall so calmly into the old routine, and Willy Erskine, after his voyage, look in to tea? She did not know if she walked on air or solid ground when she made her way down again to the pier. If that were to be the end of it, of what use had been all the agonies of those silent months? Life seemed to swim before her like a dream and confused phantasmagoria, as she thought, but yet a subtle sense of happiness was gathering at her heart. He was coming so soon; he was so near; and all those ghosts would roll up their gloomy wings and disappear out of sight, when Willy Erskine once more looked in at the Gushat-house. She went quickly down along the half-deserted road to the pier where the women were all crowding. The *Pretty Peggy* could not reach the harbour yet for more than an hour; but still, to be so much nearer her, to be ready to meet the men and hear that all was well, five minutes earlier, was compensation enough for the wives. They made pleasant little speeches to Nora as she came down among them. "Ah, Miss Nora, the day will come when you'll be lookin' out for a man o' your ain," said one. "And I hope with a'my heart it'll be a good man and a pleasant day," added another. "But Miss Nora's man will never be a seafarin' man like ours, to make her heart sair," said a third. "Unless it was a grand captain of a frigate in a' his gold lace," was the ambitious aspiration of Nancy Morrison. "Sure I am, I didna bring up a winsome young lady for less than that." She was a favourite, and this was the pleasant chatter that passed, as she went among them, from lip to lip.

"I want to see Willy come in from his first voyage, nurse," said Nora. What a lying, wicked little speech it was!—and what a true one!—but before Nancy had time to answer, one of the men on the outlook threw down his telescope with a groan—rather the glass slid out of his hands. "Get out o' my way, women, wi' your cacklin'," he said, as he stumbled down. "Oh, Lord, and their mother that canna stir a foot from her bed!" With this the old sailor turned his back on the advancing ship, and sat down on the edge of the pier, and hid his face in his hands. This action alarmed the entire community, for Peter Rodger was well known to have two sons in the *Pretty Peggy*. Two or three of the women crowded round him to ask what he meant, when another of the men gave a sudden cry. "My God, the flag's at the half-mast!" he exclaimed.

A sudden horror fell upon the group. It fell upon the town instinctively, in the twinkling of an eye; the news flew by that strange electricity which is quicker than the telegraph. It was a sunny afternoon, the Firth was like glass, the sky was blue—nothing but the white clouds above and the soft, gliding sails below disturbed the glistening surface of the sea. The ship, with its white sails, came softly on before a slight but favourable breeze; but the faces of the little crowd grew pale in the sunshine, and a shudder ran through them. There was a pause, and every heart stood still. "She's got the garland on the topmast; she's made a good voyage," said a younger sailor, under his breath. "Oh, lad, how dare ye speak," cried one of the women, "when she's bringing death maybe to your mother or to me?"

The strain of the suspense was terrible, as they stood and watched. Some of the poor wives fell on their knees and prayed aloud—as if that would bring to life the dead man, probably long ago committed to the safe-keeping of the sea; some sat down and began to rock themselves, crying silently, as if their individual fate had been sealed. As for Nancy Morrison, she stood rigid, with a face as pale as stone, and with big, dilated eyes watched the ship that was bringing her life or death. Nora was shocked and disturbed, as was natural. Her heart went forth in a certain passionate pity for the one, whoever it was, upon whom the blow was about to fall; but she did not feel the same overpowering anxiety as that which moved the others. She went softly to her old nurse, and put her arm round the poor woman. "Oh, Nancy, take courage," she cried; "don't think it's him!"

"Let me be! oh, let me be!" cried Nancy.

There was no one there in a condition to take comfort or give attention to anything but one.

And the ship came so slowly, as it seemed to everybody now. The Firth lit up with all the glorious reflections of the sunset; the May rose dark upon the blazing water, with the iron skeleton that held at night its fire signal; the Bass lay like an uncouth shell against the dim outline of land on the other side, and the long sun-rays slanted and fell tenderly across the water. Then the horrible excitement of the watchers was roused into a sharper crisis still. A boat darted forth from the shore with six stout oarsmen, to the slowly gliding ship. Could it be a ship of death, like that one that the Ancient Mariner saw against the sun? Could there have been pestilence on board? It came on gliding, as the other vessel must have done when "the men all light, the seraph men," brought her near the port. These wild thoughts passed through Nora's mind alone. There came into it a curious vague wonder whether it might have been Providence, and not she, that sent Willy Erskine into such a ship. She seemed to see him on the deck with all, or almost all, the authority in his hands—the saviour of most of the disabled crew; healer, ruler, hero. Such was the strange vision that glided before her eyes as she too eagerly watched the boat. The thought of his supposed devotion made Nora unselfish too. She ceased to tremble about their personal meeting. She kept eye and hand firm, to be ready to give help and succour to her who might be smitten, whoever she might be.

When the boat came back, and got within hailing distance, the excitement grew terrible. Some of the poor wives threw themselves among the rocks to get the news a moment earlier. Peter Rodger stood on the highest ledge, with his broad hand curved like a trumpet round his eager ear. Nora placed herself behind her nurse instinctively, for she loved the woman. But the awful strain of all their ears and senses made the first cry unintelligible to them. Twice the vague shout came over the waters before it could be comprehended. Then it was caught up and echoed by a hundred voices—"Only the doctor!" That was what they said.

Only the doctor! There was a shout, and then a cry, sharp with joy, from all those women. Joy! though it was still death that was coming. They clasped each other's hands; they wept aloud; they cried out, in the relief of their deliverance. The whole community, every living creature about, began to breathe, and babble, and sob forth thanksgiving. One figure alone fell forward against the wall on which Nancy Morrison had been leaning. Nora was stupefied. It was like a great rock falling suddenly down upon her out of the peaceful sky. She shrank, and gave one wail and shudder, and then it came, crushing the heart and flesh. The doctor! He had said true—she was never to see him more.

"Miss Nora, cheer up," said Nancy, crying, and laughing, and shivering with joy. "Dinna take it so sair to heart. It's her nerves, my bonnie woman. But they're a' safe, noo, baith lads and men. It's but the doctor—do ye no' hear what they say?"

Then Nora rose up desperate, and turned her stony face upon them. "Do you think there's none to break their hearts for him?" she cried, with a wild indignation. "Do you think there's no mother, no woman watching? Be silent, ye cruel women! How dare you tell me it's only *him*?"

Then they all looked at her with pathetic faces, gathering round her where she stood—she who did not know what she was saying. Impatiently she turned from their looks. What could sympathy or anything do for her? What did it matter? "Let me be!" she cried, as Nancy had cried. Let her alone! that was all she could say.

"Eh, Miss Nora, if we had kent the doctor was onything to you!" cried one of the pitiful women. Nora turned round with a certain wild fierceness almost before the words were said.

"And who said he was anything to me?" she asked, with a strange scorn of herself and them. He was nothing to her; she could not even wear black for him, or let anybody know she mourned. She shook herself clear of the pitying people, she could not tell how. Like a blind creature, seeing nothing, with an instinct only to get home anyhow, she went straight forward, not knowing where she placed her foot; and thus walked sightless, open-eyed, and miserable—into Willy Erskine's arms.

The cry she uttered rang in the ears of all the watching population for years after. They forgot the ship and the men who were so near at hand to gather round this curious group. Nora fell forward into her lover's arms like an inanimate thing. One shock she had borne, and it had taken all her strength—the other she could not bear. For the first time in her life she lost consciousness. The light had gone out of her eyes before—now the very breath died on her lips. Mrs. Sinclair, who had come down to the pier with him to find her child, could never be sufficiently thankful that Willy was a doctor and knew precisely what to do. He carried his love all the way along the pier, hampered by eager offers of help, and still more anxious comments of sympathy, to Nancy Morrison's cottage on the shore, his heart full of remorse and exultation. Though he had long ago forgotten his threat about the *Pretty Peggy*, still it was quite true that he had come, like a conspirator, to surprise from Nora's honest eyes, from her candid face, some revelation of her true feelings. She had so revealed them now as that they never could be denied again; and though it was not Willy's fault, he was remorseful in his tenderness. He had never set foot on the *Pretty Peggy*. He had forgotten so entirely even the use he had made of her name, that he believed, like Mrs. Sinclair, that it was kindness to her foster-brother which had taken Nora to the pier. Instead of an unprofitable visit to the Greenland seas, he had been settling himself very advantageously in an inland town, where his "connections" in the county were sure to be of use to him; and after this interval, with the mother's concurrence, had come, with sober determination not to be discouraged, to know what Nora meant, and what his fate was to be. All this Nora learnt afterwards by degrees, with wrath and happiness. The doctor who had died was a dissipated old man, of a class too common in the Greenland ships. "I kent weel that doited body could never be onything to Miss Nora," cried Nancy Morrison, drying her eyes. The mystery was cleared up in a fashion to all the admiring and sympathetic population round when Willy Erskine appeared on the scene; and yet nobody knew what it meant except Nora and he.

She was very angry and she was very happy, as we have said. But she had taken all power of resistance, had she wished to resist, out of her own hands. And the story came to the usual end of such stories, and there is nothing more to say.

FOOTNOTES:

[A] The Paraphrases are a selection of hymns always printed along with the metrical version of the Psalms in use in Scotland, and more easy, being more modern in diction, to be learned by heart.

[B] Used in Scotland in the sense of weakness of body—invalidism.